THE HIDDEN SURVIVOR

The Hidden Survivor Book 1

CONNOR MCCOY

CHAPTER ONE

HE WAS DREAMING AGAIN. He knew this because the lights were on, and then because Sarah was smiling at him, holding Clarence in her arms. The toddler was reaching out for him, giggling and squirming is his mother's grasp. He reached out to take the boy, to embrace his wife and child. The boy's little hands were warm on the bare skin of his arms. He breathed Sarah's clean scent, holding them close. But they were pulled from him, fading into the distance as he woke into the cold darkness of a harsh reality.

The cold of the night seeped in through the wool blankets, and he rolled himself tighter, trying to block the memories that flooded through him.

Sarah.

Four years on he still ached for her. He supposed he hadn't mourned properly, or the pain would have dulled. Just the fact he still dreamed of them, both alive and well, spoke to his inability to come to terms with their deaths.

He knew if he tried sleeping, he'd be haunted by his former life, but the thought of getting out of bed in the dark, lighting lanterns, stoking the fire, and worse, making his way through the frozen night to the outhouse was too much for him. He'd take on the memories. And there was a chance he'd drop back to sleep. He was sometimes lucky.

But this wasn't one of the lucky nights. Glen's mind flooded with the light of his Philadelphia home. Sarah's laughter as she met him at the end of the day. Before Clarence was born, they often dined out in the best restaurants, rubbing elbows with the movers and shakers of the city. His advances in neurosurgery bringing him acclaim and celebrity. They were invited to the mayor's home several times a year.

He re-lived that blaze of glory with something akin to envy. As if he hadn't been the one whose career was rising like a star. But it had been, and the envy was easier to handle than the loss. He still was alive after the automobile crash that had robbed him of everything he loved, but his desire to achieve, to thrive and grow, died with his wife and child. Exactly one year to the day after the crash he walked away from his surgical practice, and drove away from Philly, leaving everything behind.

But the memories remained with him as he headed north from Philadelphia, heading for Northern Michigan and the haunts of his childhood.

He drove through New York, stopping in Syracuse to trade his Lexus for an old beater of a Ford truck with a temperamental manual transmission, and rust flaking from the undercarriage. At the Canadian border, the border patrol agent looked from his enhanced driver's license to his face several times.

"Your name?" the officer asked him, watching him.

"Glen Carter," he said, forcing a smile. "I was ill and lost some weight," he explained.

"It's more what you gained," she said. "You look like a professional in your picture." She eyed him from his torn jeans to his scruffy beard and greasy hair. "Where are you headed?"

"I'm just driving through Ontario on my way to Northern Michigan. I own a cabin there." He started to fish out the deed to the cabin, but she waved him on.

"Enjoy your trip, Mr. Carter," she said as he pulled away.

He stopped out of sight of the border crossing and pulled down his visor to look in the mirror, examining his face. The border control agent had been correct. He had let himself go. It probably would be wise to look a little bit more like his ID photo when he re-entered the United States. At twilight, he rented himself a room in a budget hotel and bought a razor from the little shop.

When Glen was done showering and shaving, he looked, and felt, more like himself than he had in a long time. He'd trimmed his beard down to a neat mustache and a chin strap beard and taken his hair from shoulder length to a high and tight cut, almost military-looking, with scissors and an electric razor. He was much thinner than he used to be, but at least his face resembled the one on his ID and the ghost of the surgeon he'd once been reappeared.

He crossed the border near Sault Ste. Marie easily and drove south on Highway 75 and then west on Route 28 onto the familiar farm-lined roads of his childhood summers. Leaving behind successively smaller towns, he headed into the forested hills, relying on memory to find his way.

The track to the cabin was so overgrown that he almost missed it. Luckily, his instincts had made him slow down, almost crawling along the dirt road the track led off. But he spotted the sign dangling from a vine that had saved it from toppling into the brush along the side of the road and being hidden forever. He considered clearing the worst of the growth, but why. The truck already was dented and scratched, it wouldn't make much difference.

He bounced along the half-mile track, sliding under some tree limbs, breaking others until he reached his destination. Boarded up and abandoned years before, the cabin was not the welcoming place of his memory. The front stairs were rotted, and the dock was tilting crazily into the pond. There was a lot of work to do here.

The thought of the work heartened him. He needed something to focus his mind. Something that required his full attention. Something to take his mind off his desire to join his departed wife and child. He pulled his tool box from behind his seat and set to work pulling the plywood from the doors and windows.

Glen worked steadily through the summer months, often to the point of exhaustion. The dreams haunted him less often when his body reached the limits of its endurance. He rebuilt the front steps, repaired the listing dock, and built a shed to house the truck for the winter. Inside, he tore out the old brickwork around the fireplace, put in a wood stove and put in a firewall of native stone.

His hands became scarred, and as he assumed he never would perform surgery again, he didn't think twice about the bruises and sprains on his fingers. He dropped a stone on his hand and broke his pinky and ring finger, but didn't bother with a doctor. He swore, threatened to shoot the offending rock, and taped the fingers together until they healed.

He would not be returning to his old life.

It wasn't only the dreams that woke him at night. The first time the noise woke him he sat straight up in his bed, sure that whatever had made that hellish howl was in his cabin. He shook with adrenaline and tried formulating a plan. But when the guttural roar came again, it was clear that it was outside and moving away. He tried to calm himself, but it took ages before the shaking stopped wracking his body. He looked in the woods but didn't know what he was looking for.

Something huge. He began understanding why people believed in Big Foot and Yeti. How could there be no evidence of something that loud?

Two years into his isolation, civilization ended. When the power went out and hadn't come back on after a week, he dusted off the truck and drove to town to find out what had happened, but the place was in chaos. Cars stranded on the roads, people carrying firearms, if there were people at all. He found a woman siphoning gasoline from the storage tank at a deserted gas station and asked her what had happened.

She looked at him strangely. "Where have you been?" she asked, eyeing him suspiciously. "How can you not know?"

Glen told her he'd been holed up in the woods and she nodded, her eyes losing some, but not all, of the distrust. "Don't know for sure," she said. "It only took about a day for the entire world to go dark. Some thought a sun flare put off an EMP, but some scientist up at MIT said a sunspot wouldn't take out the whole world. We lost the radios before I ever found out for sure what took out civilization. All I know is that anything with a plug is junk. And the only people who can drive are the ones with old cars and bikes. Anything with a computer chip is toast."

"What's the fuel for?" he asked her.

"I've got a generator," she said. "Until the gasoline runs out, I've got a fridge and a freezer and light."

"Anybody still got supplies around here? Candles? A spare generator, maybe?" he asked.

"Only if you've got something to trade." She capped her gas can and rolled up her hose. "Money isn't worth anything. But if you have goods or a skill, you might be in luck," she called over her shoulder as she moved away.

"I'm a surgeon," he said to her retreating back, and she stopped. "And I can build things. Can I borrow your siphon?"

She came back slowly, her face betraying her interest. So

while he filled the truck with fuel, he probed for more information. The town government was in upheaval. They hadn't heard anything from the county, state or federal governments. How could they? No phone, TV or radio was working. The townspeople divided between two philosophies. Those that felt the need to militarize, and those who wanted a more open society.

Town meetings quickly devolved into shouting matches between the two groups.

"No ham radio operators in town?" Glen asked, handing back her hose.

She looked thoughtful. "I don't know," she said. "If there are, they haven't stepped forward. Don't ham radios need electricity to work?"

"Batteries," he said, "that could be recharged with a generator." He gestured to the fuel can she was carrying. "When fuel runs out, then a bicycle-powered recharger probably could be rigged up pretty easily. It would give you contact with the outside world. I'm having a hard time believing no one else has thought of this," he said.

"It's only been about a week," she said. "People still are waiting for the National Guard to come to the rescue."

"The National Guard is busy keeping the cities from becoming death traps. Now, can you introduce me to someone with supplies I could barter for?"

She took him to see the owner of the local hardware store. An older man with a shotgun resting on the counter in front of him. They worked out a labor for goods exchange that had Glen installing bars over the windows and door of Hal's Hardware, and in a week he was on his way back to the cabin with a tank full of gasoline, several barrels of fuel, a generator, ham radio, and lanterns. On the seat beside him in the cab rode 100-pound bags of rice, corn, and beans. He wouldn't have a variety if he wasn't successful hunting and fishing, but he wouldn't starve.

Back at the cabin he installed bars on his windows and rigged brackets on the inside of his doors to slot two-by-fours into at night. If things got bad in town, they might come looking for him, and he didn't want to be caught unawares.

In the year that followed Glen visited the town three more times, gathering more supplies. The last time he was met by armed thugs on the road into town. He wasn't surprised, he figured it would come to that eventually. He made a U-turn and decided not to go back. He parked his truck in the shed, walked back out to the road and constructed a blind to pull across the entry to his driveway. The fewer people who knew where he was, the better.

Another year went by and Glen settled into a routine. Every day of decent weather he rose at dawn and spent an hour fishing in the creek downstream from his pond. Then he chopped and stacked wood. He spent the late morning searching for signs of humanity, and was happy when none appeared. If he'd been woken in the night by the sound of what he only could assume was a wild animal, he spent some time looking for signs of bears, moose, and wolves.

There was no trace of anything that seemed large enough to emit the sounds that woke him, although he did see bear scat and trees that had been marked. He sometimes came across signs of moose, and about twice a year would see one standing in the pond or stream. He knew about the dangers of moose. A rutting bull easily could kill a man. He kept his distance.

He ate his one meal of the day mid-afternoon; if he was home he'd cook and eat a warm meal. He carried home cured jerky and foraged for edible greens, fruits and berries if his wanderings had taken him far afield. He was keeping an eye on civilization, but from a good distance. He carried his binoculars and spied on settlements. They couldn't be called towns anymore. Society had devolved. Every group he came across, large or small, was protecting itself against outsiders. Even neighboring towns that used to be filled with friends and relatives were looked upon with suspicion. The people no longer were considered family. Some bartering was tolerable, but that was all. Watching from the forest, Glen watched a woman turn her mother away. She needed something, Glen wasn't sure what, but she had nothing to give in return. Angry words were exchanged and the older woman turned away, weeping.

The younger woman gathered her children around her and herded them into the house, clearly worried about retribution. But the old woman didn't live to take revenge. The leader of her compound shot her dead when she came back empty-handed. She laid in the road until nightfall, when something came out of the woods and dragged her away.

Glen stayed away from other people as a rule, but he made a mental note never to ask the people in this valley for help. His skin crawled and a shiver went up his spine at the thought of the interactions involving the old woman. Turned away by her kin, killed and then left for the animals. One minute in the road, the next gone.

After that encounter, if it could be called an encounter, it was more like a vignette viewed from afar. He stuck close to home, not caring to see what was going on in the "civilized" world. He was perfectly content to chop wood, hunt, and fish. He had no need of the company of others. It was a lonely life, but at least he was unlikely to be killed by his companions.

CHAPTER TWO

A FOX STARTED VISITING the stream above the pond that summer. Glen spotted her standing in the shallows, drinking. Then something caught her attention and she froze, watching the water intently. A moment later she sprang, diving head first into the water and coming up with a medium-sized trout in her mouth. The fish was struggling, thrashing back and forth and the fox dropped it in the shallows. But a moment later she had snatched it up again, carrying it out of the stream and dropping it on the sandy bank.

The fox stood between the fish and the water and batted it landward with her paws and nose when it seemed it might escape back into the water. A few moments later, the struggle was over and the fox picked up the now motionless fish and trotted away.

Glen decided the fox had the right idea and grabbed his fishing gear, making his way upstream to a curve where a small watering hole had developed. It was a good place to spend an afternoon fishing. He wondered where the fox had come from, she was the first he'd seen so close to the cabin. He sat on the bank for a while before he dropped his line in, wondering at the feeling of companionship he'd felt at spotting her. He hadn't realized he neither needed nor wanted company.

When he had three good-sized trout on his line he headed back to the cabin. Two of the fish he filleted for his own consumption, but before he started on the third he paused. He wished now he'd taken a bucket and brought the trout back alive. He could have rigged a holding area in the pond and used the fish to lure the fox back to the area. If he left a dead fish on the bank now, there was no telling what animal would find it.

Probably not the fox who just had eaten.

A good part of a week went by before the fox appeared again. Glen was sitting on his deck when movement on the far bank of the pond caught his eye. He spotted the white tip of her tail as she slipped through the reeds. A moment later she appeared on a bare stretch and dipped her nose to the water for a drink. Then she sat on the bank and watched the water for a few minutes, but nothing caught her eye and she slipped back into the undergrowth.

Glen watched a while longer, but she didn't reappear. He felt oddly let down.

The next day he fashioned a small underwater holding tank using some chicken wire he'd found stored under the deck. He attached it to the dock with wire and then took his rod and bucket to his fishing hole. This time he brought back five good-sized trout alive in his bucket and dumped them into his fish cage. Then he sat on the dock to wait.

The following day, back out on the dock again, he glimpsed the fox, but she had spotted him and didn't stay. It was two more days before he saw her again. This time she appeared on the far bank and stood absolutely still, watching him. Glen moved slowly, dipping his net into the water and coming up with a trout from his tank.

The fox licked her lips.

Glen waited until the fish stopped moving and grabbed it by the tail, tossing it along the bank, as far from the dock as he could get it. The movement startled the fox and she disappeared into the undergrowth. Glen cursed under his breath. His plan hadn't worked. He was just about to get up to retrieve the fish for his own consumption when he spotted her again and lowered himself back down.

She'd appeared out of the reeds a few yards from where the fish had landed. Her gaze flicked from him to the fish and back again. She remained still for several minutes, her ears flicking back and forth, before she shot forward, seized the trout and disappeared again. Glen smiled and retreated back to the cabin.

It became a ritual. He'd head out to the pond at dusk, and every second or third day the fox would appear and wait for him to toss her a fish. He sometimes would see her on his on hunts. She'd be carrying a small mammal or bird, so he felt comfortable that she still was able to survive on her own. But she came to the pond regularly and sometimes would sit companionably on the far bank, watching him, before trotting over to her fish retrieval spot and waiting for him to feed her.

The fox never ate the fish in front of Glen. He wasn't sure if that was because she wasn't comfortable eating in front of him, or if she had kits in her den that she was feeding. But one day she was followed out of the reeds by two round and clearly well-fed kits. The vixen kept them behind her with bared teeth and growls. They were unafraid and would have wrestled and tumbled right up to Glen if she had let them.

He threw the fish, and when the kits leaped upon it and started tearing it apart he threw another for their mother. Later, when they slipped back into the undergrowth, she shot him a look, which Glen interpreted as, "I'm trusting you, don't disappoint me."

That summer the fox family regularly spent time on the river bank, the young foxes frolicking in the water, wrestling or trying unsuccessfully to catch fish, while their mother lay in the shade, watching. At first, she had kept a watchful eye on Glen, but as he never approached her family she began to relax and even would doze in the afternoon sun while Glen tended his vegetable patch or chopped wood for the winter.

Glen was sitting at his table eating rice and beans and watching the vixen teaching her kits to fish when everything changed. He was craving meat and wondering if he had over-hunted the woods around his cabin. It had been days since he'd trapped even a squirrel. He supposed he'd better plan a hunting expedition before winter set in. But he was tired. The previous night he'd been awakened by the howling. So he'd sleep tonight, prepare tomorrow, and leave the following day.

It wouldn't serve him well to set out on a several day trip in less than peak form. It would be too easy to miss something, take a wrong step, and end up dying in the forest, hobbled by a broken leg. Prime prey for some other predator, animal or human.

Movement out by the pond caught his attention. His fox, as he liked to think of her, was standing with her head up and ears forward, very still. With two flicks of her ears she turned and, yipping to the cubs, they melted into the undergrowth. Glen wondered what had startled her. A predator maybe?

He went back to making notes on the fly page of a novel, the only paper that remained in the cabin, when a knock sounded on the door. His head flew up, and at first he thought he must have imagined it, but it came again. And then the latch rattled.

Glen stood, pushing back his chair so sharply it fell over.

He stared at the door, uncertain how to proceed. The blinds on the windows at the front of the cabin were closed, but if the person or persons walked around back, he'd be vulnerable. The back wall was largely windows, affording a view onto the back deck overlooking the pond. It was peaceful and beautiful and if he'd had any brains we would have boarded up those windows. They had no blinds.

"Please help us." A woman's voice pleaded from the other side of the door. "Our friend is injured. Oh, please." The knocking devolved into a slapping of palms against the wood. The woman was sobbing, whimpering "please," over and over again.

Glen remembered the old woman turned away by her daughter, killed by the people she had lived with. Did he want to lower himself to that level of inhumanity? He took a step toward the door and then another. He picked his rifle out of the stand by the door and checked to see if it was loaded. The slapping at the door stopped.

He jumped when the knocking started again. It had a different quality this time, more like a hammering. Whoever was pounding now had something that could be used as a weapon. Metal and heavy. He readied his rifle, pulled the bolt back and, blocking the door with his shoulder, cracked it open.

"Oh, thank God," a tall reedy brown-haired woman choked out. She stood behind a blonde woman with a metal flashlight she'd been using to hammer on the door, and behind them both a man was slumped against the post holding up the porch roof, holding his arm across his gut and covered with blood from the waist down. As Glen watched, he slowly slid to the porch floor, tilting crazily as he tried to maintain a sitting position.

The brown haired woman had wild eyes, and was shaking, clearly unable to control herself. She was choking back sobs and had a hand held over her mouth. The shorter blonde woman looked detached, which could be a sign of shock as well, but also could mean she wasn't invested in the others and just didn't care. Glen thought he caught a glimpse of anger in there as well.

The man's face was covered with a sheen of sweat. He clearly was in a lot of pain, judging by the amount of blood he'd lost. He was staying conscious only by extreme effort and it was taking its toll on him. Glen thought they only had a small window of time before he became deadweight.

Glen carefully unloaded the rifle and set it back in its cradle, leaving the door wide open, because once he'd made the decision to help they were coming in anyway. "Help me," he croaked to the shorter woman, the one who'd been glaring at him, but was able to keep her shit together. The other one had begun sobbing the minute he'd opened the door.

They supported the groaning man between them, pulling him up and helping him into the cabin. He was soaked in blood and left a trail of it behind them.

"Clear off the low table," he barked at the sobbing woman, the words coming out as a croak. It had been so long since he'd spoken to anyone.

She grabbed the coffee cup and swept the books onto the floor so that Glen could lay the man on the table. He looked up from the man, gauging which of the women might be able to help, and noticed the tall brown-haired woman was pale, sweating and shaking.

"What is your name?" he asked, his voice still rough from disuse.

"S-S-Sally," she stuttered. "Sally Winter."

"Sally Winter, you are suffering from shock. I need you to lie down on the couch with your feet raised on the arm, and pull that blanket over you." He motioned to the wool blanket hanging over the back of the couch. "Okay. Can you do that for me?"

Sally nodded and collapsed on the couch. The other woman pushed her down and lifted her feet onto the arm of the couch before pulling the blanket over her. Sally was sobbing softly, trying to calm herself, with little success.

Glen looked for the short blonde. She was standing by the windows looking out at the pond. She didn't seem at all distressed by her companions' condition.

"Blondie," he said rudely, hoping to shake her out of her lethargy. "I need you to come here."

She turned and complied, a slightly puzzled look on her face. "Are we going to help him die?" she asked. "Because I'm pretty sure he's not going to recover from this."

"Then why did you bring him here?" Glen asked sharply. "I'm a surgeon, and I might be able to save him, but I'll need your help. What's your name?

"Mia," she said. "What do you need me to do?"

"First, grab the whiskey from the cupboard over the sink, and get some down, Sally."

While Mia went to rummage for whiskey and glasses in the kitchen, Glen busied himself with rolling a towel to put underneath the man's head and fetching a blanket for covering his arms and chest. When Mia had done as he asked he said, "See the door on the left down that hall? It's the bathroom. Look in the tall cabinet for the sterile saline. Grab that and a box of sterile gauze." Glen turned his attention back to the man and noticed Sally watching him. She had the blanket clutched up under her chin.

"What's his name?" he asked her.

"Christian," she said. "Chris."

Glen nodded and turned back to his patient. Chris was watching him dully, no hope or expectation in his eyes.

"I'll do my best for you, Chris, but it's going to hurt, and I need you to lie as still as possible. Okay?"

Christian nodded his head and squeezed his eyes shut. Mia came back in the room with the saline and gauze and Glen nodded to a lamp table nearby.

"Drag that over, and put the supplies on it."

She did so, intelligently placing the table where the light from the oil lantern would do the most good, setting the supplies neatly in a row next to it. Whatever else Mia was, she had a calm head on her shoulders.

"Now back into the bathroom," he said. "On the shelf above where you found the saline there is a medical kit. Use both hands, and carry it level – just like it is on the shelf. Everything is sterile, and the lid has a nasty habit of popping off if you aren't careful. Bring that here," Glen said.

He turned back to his patient. He'd put off the inspection of the wounds for far too long. He unbuttoned what remained of Chris's flannel shirt and pulled it aside, tugging gently to remove the shreds of fabric from the wounds. Chris held himself rigid, a moan escaping clenched teeth.

The wounds were deep and looked to Glen as if Chris had been both clawed and bitten. His experience as a neurosurgeon didn't exactly prepare him for the scope of damage to Chris's torso. In addition to the gaping slashes made by claws, there was a chunk missing from his lower abdomen and puncture wounds from teeth, which were going to be difficult to close in these circumstances.

Glen picked up a bottle of saline, broke the seal and dumped it in the wounds to wash them out. Chris screamed and passed out.

CHAPTER THREE

IN RETROSPECT it made sense that governing bodies around the world kept the news of the Space Storm quiet. They were running solution scenarios and didn't need their people panicking, stampeding, or blaming whomever for the impending disaster. Why have to deal with rioting civilians if you didn't have to do so? The consequence, of course, was that no one was prepared.

When the news starting leaking in the weeks before the Earth traveled through the pocket of radiation that the news outlets had named Space Storm Agatha, people went into high gear. There was a run on survival supplies, and when the stores sold out, the thefts began. In one town a group of citizens broke into an old EMI warehouse and stole everything usable. Unfortunately, the supplies had been designated for the National Guard in their effort to assist those who were hardest hit after the storm passed.

Those supplies never were recovered.

But in the end, it didn't really matter. Everyone was hard hit. Only those who'd been preparing for an EMP for many years were better off than anyone else. Unless you counted the uber rich, who were able to buy anything they wanted. They were set until their fuel ran out.

Every morning Glen brewed himself a pot of strong coffee, which he would consume while listening to the radio. At first the news was puzzling. There were rumors of an impending disaster. People who studied ancient texts were coming out of the woodwork, volunteering to tell what they knew to every TV and radio station in the world. They pointed out the signs, repeated that, through the ages, there had been a cyclical pattern of encounters with the Space Storm.

Of course, the effects weren't so damaging before electricity. Radiation sickness killed some cattle, and some children were born with deformities. But whole civilizations didn't collapse. One show devolved into a shouting match between two self-proclaimed prophets regarding details so trivial as to be meaningless.

The scientific community had as much trouble coming to a consensus as the prophets. One set believed the Space Storm would pass with as much fuss as the much-hyped millennial computer system crash that never came to pass. According to scientific expert Tom Flannery, there was no reason to expect any negative effects from the small amount of radiation emanating from the cloud.

But if you listened to EMP expert Nolan French, you'd know to build yourself a Faraday cage and put any electronics safely in it. He suggested transforming your garage into a Faraday cage so your vehicle would be drivable after we passed through the Space Storm. Glen lined a garbage can with cardboard, tossed in his two-way radios, his spare computer, rechargeable batteries, and a solar charger. He backed up photos of Sarah and Clarence onto a flash drive and dropped that and a drive with his music into the can. Then he sealed it all with aluminum tape.

His generator presented larger problems. He wasn't interested in traveling into town to find a box. So he built a wooden platform over a sheet of metal and stuck the generator on it. Then he built a box around it. He used glue instead of nails or screws. And then surrounded the wooden box with aluminum foil that he taped to the metal base. It may or may not work, but he wouldn't know until the Space Storm had passed. And truthfully, what use would all that stuff in the can be if there wasn't any kind of Internet or electricity available? Just a fancy way to look at pictures of his family or listen to music, really.

The voices on the radio got more frantic every day leading up to the event. It was unclear if the radiation would be harmful to humans. People in the cities planned to ride out the storm underground. In rural America, root and storm cellars were made ready. People were hunkering down, gathering supplies, and even boarding up windows. Glen wasn't sure what good that would do, but if it made people feel better, then why not? The world was going into hiding.

Except for those on the fringe. There were always nutjobs who had to do it differently. There were groups of people making plans to party on the highest buildings in the cities, up Half Dome, or on the beach. He heard what sounded like a Valley Girl talking animatedly about how she was going to a party on the roof of the Wilshire Grand Center in Los Angeles, unless the party at the beach was going to be more fun. She was having a terrible time deciding which one to go to.

Glen's plan was to stay inside. If there were caves nearby, that would have been his choice, but there were not. He was staying off the roads, which were bound to be populated by idiots of one sort or another. He would stay put. Anyway, it was likely a bunch of excitement about nothing, like the year 2000 all over again.

He'd opened his Faraday cage and set his spare, battery-powered radio in it before taping it up again, berating himself even as he used the last of his aluminum tape. If the power went out, there would be no radio stations to listen to, would there? He did it anyway, feeling vaguely foolish.

The morning of the end found Glen with his cup of coffee and the radio on. Every station was covering the event. On PBS the local broadcaster was on the road.

"I'm headed east on I-64 and it's a bright morning. It's hard to believe we'll be knee deep in space dust in another hour or so. The road is spooky. There just isn't any traffic anywhere. Except, Christ! A car just passed me going so fast it had to be over one hundred miles per hour. Where's he going in such a hurry? Or she? To be fair, it could have been a woman. They were going too fast to tell."

That hour passed, and Glen stayed locked on the radio.

"The sky is showing some interesting signs." The reporter was subdued now. Tense. "There are reports of aurora borealis in some of the strangest places. This must be the cause of the radiation in this cloud. The governments of the world are encouraging people to stay inside. The "Space Storm" should pass in about two hours."

Glen looked outside of his cabin to find the sky changing from its typical midday blue to a darker, almost dirty pink color. His station went dead, and he spun the dial, listening for any sign of life.

"We now are seeing the full effects of this "storm." We have lost communications with nearly everyone we were talking with." Glen didn't know who this was, but it was all he had, so he listened. "I think we have experienced effects like that of an electromagnetic pulse. Lucky for you listeners I am broadcasting from deep in the Earth," and then his radio went dead.

Glen didn't dare pull the spare radio from his Faraday cage, so he sat in silence for the rest of the day, watching the

Northern lights flicker and undulate as if they were alive. He knew the scientists had predicted they'd be out of the cloud in two hours, but if the Northern lights were any indication, the scientists had been wrong. He wasn't leaving the house until the sky went back to normal.

He stayed inside for two days, watching the sky, the woods, and the pond. No fish floated to the surface of the water and birds still were flying. That was good news. The radiation hadn't been strong enough to kill on contact. In fact, once the sky went back to normal, there wasn't much to show that the Earth had encountered a space storm at all. Only the lack of electricity.

He'd pulled out the radio and spent time every morning listening, but even the last person he'd heard, who'd claimed to be deep underground, was gone. Of course, if the transmitters had been fried, then it wouldn't matter how safe the radio operator's equipment was, there'd be no way to get the signal out. Still, every morning, Glen twirled the dial, listening for signs of life.

It wasn't until his foray into the town, when he'd worked for the ham radio, that he began hearing voices again. And what he heard chilled him. Widespread looting. Martial law declared in the cities. People dying in hospitals that no longer could help them.

The cities were running out of fuel quickly. The generators that kept medicines chilled and medical equipment functioning were falling silent. People who thought solar or wind power would save them were disappointed when the diodes that controlled delivery were fried.

Those people who actually were prepared hunkered down and didn't open their gates to strangers. If you weren't already part of their plan, it was too late now. Those preppers who knew to keep their solar and wind equipment in a Faraday cage were not about to save the people who didn't.

Glen listened to stories of people trapped in elevators, on amusement park rides and in planes falling from the sky. Not commercial planes, because every government everywhere grounded the commercial flights. But that didn't stop private plane owners from taking flight and falling from the sky. Not all of them, because like older cars, older airplanes operated without electronics. There was apparently some spectacular footage filmed with a super eight camera, but there was no way to disseminate it except at a private viewing at the camerawoman's home using a crank projector. The stories skipped across the country, often becoming so distorted that they were no longer recognizable to the people who had lived the experience.

Glen's own life was little changed from before the event. Electricity had been a luxury for a cabin originally built off-grid. He had his generator, but rarely used it except for when he felt the need for hot water. He kept food cold in buckets with watertight lids, weighted and sunk to the bottom of the pond. As autumn waned and ice started to form on the surface, he pulled his refrigerator buckets out of the water and kept them in an insulated shed instead. He built a cache on the roof of the shed to keep items that would survive freezing, like the venison he hunted.

As the days grew colder and he had less to keep him occupied outside, his thoughts drifted to his family. He knew Sarah would be disappointed that he wasn't out in the world, helping people. She would have visited every family within a two-day walk to offer her services to anyone with a need. She would have created community, not isolated herself in this cabin.

Sarah would have gone to town and stayed. Working to build community, to reboot society. She would have been asking questions about what it would take to get the power back on, not taking for granted that it couldn't be done. He felt vaguely ashamed of himself, hiding out here in his cabin, licking his wounds.

He thought about visiting the town again, but something didn't feel right. He did not think he'd be welcome. Yes, he was a surgeon, but they had doctors there. Anyone who needed his specialty would not be likely to live anyway. Not without electricity, anesthesia, and antibiotics.

"I'm sorry, Sarah," he said aloud. "There just isn't any point in it."

For a moment he thought he heard her voice. "And what's the point in living if you aren't helping others?"

He shook his head. She would never not be with him. He knew exactly what she would say and the tone she would use. A wry smile twisted his mouth. Isolating himself up here only had lodged her more tightly in his mind. He hadn't forgotten at all. He saw now that if he'd wanted to forget, escaping had been a mistake. It was contact with the living world that would have dulled the pain and faded the memories.

Maybe that was the real reason he'd come up here. To keep his family more firmly with him.

He started talking to Sarah and Clarence more often, explaining to the boy what he was doing as he tracked rabbits in the snow. Teaching him how to set a trap, to bait a hook, to be still and listen. In the evening he would tell Sarah what he'd been doing during the day, the interesting or horrifying things he had seen. What he thought about the world.

When the fox came into his life, he shared her with his wife and son. Explaining to Clarence how he was taming the creature, sharing with Sarah why he bothered.

"Remember how we always said we'd have a dog someday, Sarah? It's like that, but better. She's a dog, a companion, but she doesn't need me. If something happens and I'm not here for a while, she can take care of herself. She's not reliant on me, but she's sharing her life with me."

In his mind, Sarah smiled. She understood how important companionship was.

It was during the first snow after the lights went out, when Glen was showing Clarence his favorite spot for watching the valley, that he made a mistake. He climbed to the high overlook, telling Clarence to watch for the hawk that nested nearby. He stepped up onto the rock ledge where he liked to sit, not realizing the snow was hitting the rock and icing it over. If his first step had slipped, he would have been okay, but that spot must not have iced over, because he didn't slip. It was the second step, after he was committed to the ledge that did him in.

His left foot slid out from under him. He scrambled to right himself, but he was well and truly on the ice now and he could not regain his balance. He fell, striking his head, and slid over the edge, falling to an outcropping a good fifteen feet below. He was unconscious when he landed.

He woke at dusk, the sharp sound of a high bark pulling him back to consciousness. The world was out of focus when he opened his eyes and it took him a few minutes to understand what he was seeing. On the ledge above him the fox stood looking down. She yipped once more and disappeared.

Glen sat up carefully. He put a hand to the back of his head and it came away warm and sticky with blood. He was dizzy, but light was fading, so he got unsteadily to his feet and examined the rock face. He thought he heard Clarence crying and hastened to reassure him.

"It's okay, Bud," he said. "I'll be fine. This looks worse than it is." And he meant not only his head but also the rock face, which looked as smooth as glass.

CHAPTER FOUR

GLEN SEARCHED the cliff face for another moment, trying to see a way up, but moving his head made him dizzy. So, he sat back down and closed his eyes, trying to regain his equilibrium. A moment later he slumped over and curled up on the ground in a fetal position.

His thoughts whirled. Would he die of blood loss if he didn't figure out a way off this ledge? What if he couldn't? What if he figured out how to get back to the top, but was too weak and dizzy to manage it? Maybe this was it. He would bleed to death here in the wilderness and birds would pick his body clean. Maybe that was what he really wanted.

He wondered idly if there was life after death. Would he join his family or just drift off into nothingness? Did it matter? He mentally bowed to the inevitable and let unconsciousness take him.

Glen did not die. That would have been too easy. He regained consciousness at dawn with the fox staring down at him and vocalizing. When his eyes opened she stopped the low growling yowl and started yipping.

"Okay, already," he muttered, his voice tight with cold. "I'm getting up."

But getting up proved to be difficult. He still was dizzy, and his body hurt like a SOB, so he started by sitting. He let the world stop spinning before he attempted to stand. Standing took several tries, and he had to brace himself against the rock wall for what seemed like an eternity with his heart beating in his ears before he was able start thinking about how to get to the top of the cliff.

He slid his hand along the wall, feeling for any irregularity that might give him a handhold or foothold. There was nothing. He tried looking for a way down, but the ledge he was on jutted out and when he looked down he couldn't even see the cliff immediately below. It was a far drop to an area with vegetation that might break his fall.

He sat on the edge with his legs dangling for a while. His head pounded and he was finding it difficult to motivate himself. He should be panicking, but his give-a-damn appeared to be broken. He stared off into space, letting his mind drift.

It was hunger that brought him back. His stomach grumbled and he felt slightly sick. How long had it been since he'd eaten? He looked around for something to curb the hunger and that's when he noticed there was a tree growing from the other side of an outcropping. He'd been standing too close to the cliff to notice it before.

He slid back from the edge and got to his feet. The dizziness had abated somewhat. He went to the far edge of the ledge where an outcropping blocked his view to the right and narrowed the ledge to a sliver of just a few inches. He slid down next to the outcropping and slid along the ledge, trying to see around. But his body was too big for the narrow ledge and he had to slide back before he could see what lay beyond.

He stood and, flattening his body against the cliff face, he inched along, sliding his feet along the narrow ledge while pressing his chest against the stone of the outcropping. His fingers felt along the wall, his arm extended, so when he found the far edge he was able to gain purchase and slide along until he could see around the edge.

There was a tree there, growing out of a crevice.

Later, he wasn't able to explain how he made it from his perilous perch, his feet barely on the ledge, to hugging the trunk of the tree with his feet scrambling for purchase. He pulled himself with trembling arms into the crook made by the trunk of the tree growing from the cliff. Later he was able to hoist himself up the wall by wedging his legs against the trunk and scraping his back up the rock until he could reach the top and scramble to safety.

There was no sign of the fox on his way back to the cabin, not even a print in the mud near the water. He wondered if he'd been hallucinating when he saw her staring over the cliff, barking at him. That wasn't beyond the realm of possibility.

It was while he was building a fire to heat the cabin that something he'd seen while staring out over the valley came to mind. He'd seen smoke rising from the forested hills, much closer to his home that it should have been. He'd have to keep an eye out. Maybe chase the interlopers away. Sarah would disapprove, but she'd disapprove more if he died. He must be cautious.

Once the fire was going he went to fetch some water to heat up for washing the injury on the back of his head. He cut the hair from around the wound the best that he could before scrubbing it. It was painful and began bleeding again, but he needed it to be clean. He examined it the best he could using two mirrors. It could use some stitches, but he didn't think he was up to sewing up the back of his own head and went in search of his surgical glue.

He sat in front of the fire, his head newly bandaged, with

whiskey in a glass beside him. He'd downed some painkillers but he was counting on the alcohol to take the edge off. He was fairly sure he'd cleaned the wound sufficiently, so as long as he healed without infection he'd eventually be fine. No doubt he'd suffered a concussion.

He knew he needed to rest, to let his brain recover from the trauma, but the thought of strangers on his doorstep unsettled him. He'd go out tomorrow and see what he could find out. For now he would rest. That was the best he could do.

Glen woke the next morning with a pounding head and aching body. He stripped for a bucket bath and was shocked when caught his reflection in the mirror. He had more bruised skin than not and there were cuts and scratches everywhere.

He washed, dried and then bandaged the cuts that had reopened. Then he sat on the bed and contemplated the wisdom, or lack thereof, of traveling in his condition. The camp was probably ice cold and the people gone. On the other hand, they could be sneaking up on him as he sat there in his boxers.

"Fuck it."

He began pulling on his clothes.

He took his time, moving quietly and circling the spot from where he'd seen the smoke coming in the opposite direction. He didn't want to draw attention to his cabin if he could help it. The dizziness left over from his fall still plagued him and he had to be extra careful not to trip on rocks or downed tree limbs. It took a couple of hours to find the spot and he was tired and dizzy when he caught sight of the smoke.

He hunkered down against a tree that he thought was a fifteen-minute walk from the camp. He was too tired to approach silently. He still was dizzy, and he hurt all over. He had to catch his breath at the very least. He let his chin drop to his chest.

He woke with a shotgun barrel resting against his chest. He tracked the shaft of the gun with his eyes, letting the near parts come into focus before moving on. There was a woman on the heel of the stock, her face set into a hard mask. Behind her stood a child of maybe eight years old.

He couldn't tell at first if the child was a girl or boy. For one thing it was filthy, for another the dirty blonde hair was of that indeterminate length that easily could be worn by either sex. The clothes weren't any help as they were the unisex uniform of children everywhere, jeans and a T-shirt.

"What are we going to do, Mom?" the child asked.

"Hush, Brian," she said, her gaze never leaving Glen's face.

So, it was a boy. Okay, he could work with that.

"It's okay, Brian," he said quietly. "I'm not going to hurt your mom."

The woman poked him with the rifle. "Don't speak to my son," she said grimly. "What are you doing here?"

"I saw the smoke from your campfire and came to offer assistance," Glen said. It only was a partial lie, but it still tweaked his conscience.

"What sort of assistance do you think you could provide?" she asked. "Your head is bleeding and you clearly aren't in any shape to help with much more than killing ants."

"Killing ants is important too." He surprised himself with the joke. He hadn't realized he had any sense of humor left.

"What are you really doing here?" She poked the gun into his chest again.

He pushed the barrel aside.

"I came to see who was camping on my doorstep and determine if you were a threat or not. Unfortunately, I had a mishap a few days ago and I have a concussion. It's making staying alive a little more complicated." He felt the bandage on the back of his head. She was right, it was bleeding again. "What are you doing here?" he asked.

"We are just passing through," she said. "I heard there was a doctor in this area, a doctor who isn't affiliated with a community. Would you know anything about that?"

"Why a doctor who isn't affiliated with a community?" he asked. "Wouldn't any doctor do?"

She looked at him with open contempt. "Women who need the services of a community doctor are required to perform certain acts as payment. And not just for the doctor, for the leaders of the community and anyone those leaders wish to favor. An unaffiliated doctor may ask for those same services, but at least it's only with one man." Her eyes flicked to where her son was standing. "I actually was hoping the doctor was a woman. There might be more payment options available."

Glen looked at the ground. He'd stayed away from the towns as much as possible and hadn't dwelled on what life might be like there. Women and children would be especially vulnerable to the kind of brutality that developed under rule by might.

"What do you need a doctor for?" he asked.

"That's something I'll discuss when I find one. Do you know where the doctor is?"

"I might," he said. "What are you going to do after you find your doctor?"

"We are traveling north. There are rumors of a Canadian city that still has power, and the talk is that the Canadian towns without power are much more civil places to be. They don't have the same need to rule by brutality." She glanced at the boy again. "So, do you know where to find the doctor?"

"I am the doctor," he said, tired of the guessing game. "At least I assume I'm the doctor you heard about. I'm the only person I know living outside a community in these parts."

"So, you are the doctor?" She looked ill at ease. "Brian," she said, "go up to camp and feed the fire for me, okay?"

"Are you sure, Momma?" he asked. "You said we should never be apart."

"It's okay just this once," she said. "I'll be with you in just a minute."

She watched the boy walk away before turning to Glen.

"I need an abortion," she said, her body language defiant.

"Are you sure?" he asked.

"Am I sure I'm pregnant? Yes, I'm sure. Am I sure I want an abortion? Before this, I was a member of a community. Brian needed medical care. I have no way of knowing whose baby I'm carrying, even if I was willing to bring another child into this hellhole." She looked defiant, almost daring him to comment.

"I'm not that kind of doctor, but I think I can help you," he said, although privately he had misgivings. So many things could go wrong.

"Can we take care of payment now, then?" she asked. "No point in getting rid of one baby just to create another."

"I don't want to accept sex for payment," he said, "but you can help me with my head. Does that sound like a fair trade?"

She looked surprised and a little taken aback. "Really? You don't accept sexual favors as payment? That's a first. Yes, I'll help you with your head. I suppose you mean that nasty wound you've only got partially covered."

It was his turn to be surprised. He'd thought he'd done a pretty thorough job of covering the split on his head, but he put his hand up to find the bandage had slipped.

"Yes," he said. "It looks like I'm not that great at fixing myself up."

"How did you do that?" she asked. "It's pretty nasty."

"Lost my balance on the top of the cliff, spent the night passed out on the ledge. Gave myself a concussion and I'm lucky to be alive." He flashed her his best sardonic smile. "Not sure if it's a good thing or bad thing to still be alive. The world's gone nuts."

"You can't be a positive force for change if you're dead," she said. "Where do you want to take care of our mutual problems?"

"We should retrieve your son and go back to my cabin. There's no point in trying to work out here, and I don't have everything I need for you." He pushed himself up to his feet. "Come on." He turned back to face her. "What is your name?" he asked.

"Margaret," she said. "And yours?"

"Glen." Telling her his name made him paranoid, which annoyed him. There was no reason for it. But it bothered him that he hadn't thought to give her a false one.

He took them back to the cabin, taking an even more secure route than the one that had led him to them. It was a long hike. He kept his eyes on the boy, watching for signs of fatigue. He didn't want to get them to his cabin only to have them be too exhausted to leave again. They were heading north, and while he didn't believe there was a Canadian city that still had power, the fact that they were going was fine with him.

On the way, he thought about the best ways to end a pregnancy. He could perform a D&C if necessary, but he'd rather not. He considered the medications he'd stockpiled and the plants that still might be thriving next to the river. Then he remembered the medications he'd gotten for Sarah before they had decided to keep the baby. He had never disposed of them. They probably were past their expiration dates, but that didn't mean they wouldn't be effective.

It was dusk when they returned to the cabin. Glen put together a meal of baked beans and bread. Brian ate like a boy who hadn't seen food in a year, but Margaret merely picked at her food, offering Brian most of what was on her plate. When they had finished eating he showed Margaret the bedroom and told her to put the boy to sleep on the couch. She was going to need the bedroom for privacy and her medical needs.

They did the dishes together in companionable silence, neither one displaying any impatience, both slightly anxious about what was to come. With the dishes cleaned, dried and put away he fetched his first aid kit from the cabinet in the bathroom. Then he sat on the edge of his coffee table so she would have access to the back of his head.

"I need you to make sure the wound is clean, and I'd ask you to stitch it, but unless by some small miracle you're a nurse, I think gluing is probably better."

"Not a nurse," she said, "so gluing is probably it."

She was efficient and the pain was minimal. She'd cleaned and glued, and then she was doing something else.

"What's up?" He asked. "What are you doing?"

"I read how doctors are twisting, weaving and gluing hair across head wounds to keep the edges from splitting apart. That's what I'm doing."

"Where'd you read that?" he asked. She was right, of course, he had done it himself. They used to shave the area around an incision before neurosurgery, but someone had introduced the new technique and it worked well.

"There," she said. "That looks pretty good. I mean, I've never done it before, but it looks like it'll hold."

"Thank you," he said. "Now you."

She suddenly looked nervous, hugging her arms tightly across her body. "This won't kill me, will it? Brian needs me." She looked about ready to flee.

"No, it won't kill you. When my wife got pregnant she wasn't sure she wanted to keep the baby, so I obtained some drugs. We didn't use them." He returned the first aid kit to the bathroom cupboard and rummaged around until he found what he needed on the top shelf, in the back. Just where he'd left them.

He sat on the edge of the tub remembering how he and Sarah had come here to decide. And how he hidden the pills so she wouldn't take them on impulse until they'd come to their joint decision. The memories of the joy and the sex washed over him, taking his breath away.

"Where's your wife now?" Margaret was standing in the doorway, watching him with concern on her face.

"Dead. They are both dead."

"At the end of civilization?" she asked.

"No. Before that." He avoided looking directly at her face. He couldn't deal with pity. "Car crash. They died, I lived."

"I'm sorry," she said. "But at least they aren't having to live through this."

"True," he said, but it had been difficult thinking that it was better to be dead. What if he'd died, and they were here by themselves? That might be worse.

"Can we get on with it?" she asked, motioning to the pills in his hand.

"What?" He was momentarily confused by the change of subject. "Of course."

He followed her into the main room.

CHAPTER FIVE

CHRISTIAN WAS OUT COLD, lying face up on the coffee table with a fractured wrist and a huge gash in his stomach, but little else was seriously wrong with him. Small cuts and scratches and some bruising, but nothing life-threatening, although that gash was bad news. It was ragged and black with blood. Who knew what germs were festering there?

It didn't look as though any internal organs had been damaged, but how could he be sure? His living room was not an operating room. Although the large sturdy coffee table served as a makeshift surgical table, the light barely was adequate. It wasn't sterile and there was no nurse to hold the edges of the wound apart while he poked around inside. Would he even remember what a normal liver or intestine looked like? He supposed he would know if they'd be sliced by a claw. That would be obvious enough if he actually could see anything in there.

He doused the area with antiseptic and antibiotic powder and began stitching the torn edges of muscle and skin together, layer by layer. The man groaned, but didn't regain consciousness, thank God. All he needed was his patient thrashing around while he was trying to close his wound.

The mousey woman was over by the window, weeping, the other was watching him intently as he worked. Was she trying to learn how to stitch wounds or making sure he didn't intentionally kill her friend? Maybe a bit of both.

It took a long time to complete the job. By the time he was satisfied with his work he sat up to find he was stiff. The weeping woman had stopped, thank God. Hopefully, she could keep her shit together until they could leave.

But that wouldn't be soon. The young man would need rest and time for healing. If he started off too soon, the chances of tearing open the stitches would be high.

"Help me," he ordered the women. "I need to tape a dressing to this wound, and then we should move him to the couch."

"Okay, what do you need me to do?" the one who had been watching stepped around the couch. Mia, he thought.

"Wash your hands in the sink there." He pointed to the kitchen. "Then you can cut medical tape for me. There's a towel in the drawer to the left of the sink."

Glen set out the sterile dressing while Mia did as she was told and came back with clean dry hands. She took the tape and scissors and made precise cuts just where he told her. He took the tape from her and sealed the dressing to Christian's abdomen.

When he was done he said, "We need to move him to the couch, and it's going to take all three of us."

Sally threw him a startled look and he thought she might bolt. But she pulled herself together and approached.

"I need two clean sheets from the hall cupboard," he said. "Top sheets."

A moment later he could hear her rifling through the cupboard and she came back with two sheets.

He nodded to the couch. "Put one of them on there, give me the other."

She handed him a sheet and set to work tucking the other around the cushions of the couch.

Glen unfolded his and smoothed it onto the coffee table next to Christian. "You," he said to Mia, "come here and help me."

"I guess what they say about doctors is true," Mia said.

"What you mean by that?" Glen asked.

"So full of their own importance that they don't think to use basic courtesy." She raised an eyebrow at him.

He felt his cheeks flush and was annoyed that she had gotten to him. "I'm going to roll Christian onto his side," he said. "Can you please," he emphasized the please, "shove that half of the sheet as far under him as you can? There needs to be an excess under him. Okay?"

She nodded, and he rolled the man up onto his side. Mia gave a startled look at his biceps and then quickly and efficiently bunched the sheet up under Christian.

"Okay, good, thank you." He said, annoyed at how self-conscious he'd become about his language. "Now I'm going to roll him onto his other side and I need you to pull the sheet out from underneath him and across the coffee table. Not the whole sheet, just enough that we easily can move him from the table to the couch. Am I clear?"

She nodded and he felt his biceps bunch again as he rolled Christian onto his other side. The boy groaned and tried pushing Glen away, but Mia shushed him as she pulled the sheet across the table.

"This next part is going to take all three of us," Glen said. He walked around the back of the couch and pushed it up against the coffee table. "Christian is a big guy. This isn't going to be easy. I will take his shoulders. Mia and Sally, you each can take a corner of the sheet at his feet. We will lift him up as much as we can and slide him onto the couch. Do you think you can manage?"

"Of course," Mia said.

Sally nodded, but looked doubtful.

"You can do it," Glen said to her. "It's just a moment of effort. That's all. You just have to focus and try not to drop him." He gathered the sheet in his hands near Christian's shoulders, twisting the corners to create a sling for his head. The women each wound their hands in their end of the sheet and looked at him expectantly.

"Okay, on three. One, two, three." They lifted and slid Christian over onto the couch. There was a sticking moment when his butt, being the low point, caught in the space between the table and the couch. But Glen heaved upward and they were able to get him settled.

Christian made noises of complaint and then subsided.

Glen took a moment to clean the blood from the coffee table and then motioned to the women to join him in the kitchen.

"He's going to need antibiotics," Glen said. "I think I have enough to give him a shot now, but he's going to need a full course to survive. I don't have that kind of supply."

This is not strictly true. Glen did have a stack of antibiotics in a separate cold box, but he needed to keep those for himself. If his fall from the outlook had taught him anything, it was that he needed to take care of himself first and foremost. He wasn't using up his stash of penicillin on a stranger.

Sally's face crumpled, and she began sobbing. "Where are we going to get antibiotics?" she asked through her tears.

"You could try bartering in one of the towns," he said.

"We don't have anything to barter," Mia said. "The best we can do is to steal some." And Sally sobbed even harder.

"You could try asking nicely," he said, but then remembered Margaret, and cut his sentence short. "I might be able to figure out a way to help you," he added.

Sally completely melted at this. She dropped to her knees on the kitchen floor with her hands over her face. Glen was at a loss. Why would an offer to help cause her to totally lose it? It was supposed to make her feel better.

Mia knelt and put her arm around Sally, making soothing noises.

"It's not right," Sally sobbed. "He's offering to help us and we're planning on killing him. We're not human anymore we're just animals."

"Just doing what we need to stay alive like everyone else," Mia said. "No one's human anymore."

"What are you talking about?" Glen asked.

Mia looked up with an expression of defiance on her face. "Before Christian got mauled," she said, "the plan was to rob you blind. And, if you resisted, we'd kill you. Not very nice, but it's what we do now."

"You killed people?" Glen asked casually. He didn't really believe it.

"No," Sally choked out. "Not yet. But Christian was teaching us what to do. We mostly just loot houses and camps. You were going to be our first home invasion."

"I see," he said, beginning to be thankful for the bear that had mauled Christian. "Tell me the story from the beginning. Where were you when the lights went out?" He grimaced inwardly at the cliché, but at least it got the message across.

"Chicago," Sally said. "We were living in Chicago, but we didn't know each other yet. I stayed home for a while, until the canned goods ran out and I went to a shelter. I met Mia and Christian there."

"I met Christian at a different shelter," Mia said. "But there was some trouble and we had to move. We ended up at the same place Sally was and that's how we met her."

"And were you living in Chicago too?" Glen asked.

Mia nodded. "The outskirts," she said. "I went to the shelter when the food ran out, same as Sally. Christian was there and he recruited me. There was trouble because Christian was teaching me how to rob people and I wasn't very good at it. I'm better at smash and grab than pickpocketing. Stealth makes me nervous and there was always so many people around."

"They enlisted me to help," Sally said. "I turned out to be better at lifting purses and pickpocketing, but there isn't really a point in lifting purses and wallets. Money isn't worth anything. Gold, silver and precious gems still have value, but most people want fuel, weapons, and ammunition."

"And sex," Mia said. "Women are in demand. But you must be careful. There aren't that many free women left. Most of us are owned and traded. Most men distrust free women."

"I had heard that," Glen said, once again thinking of Margaret. He wondered briefly if she'd made it to her destination. He doubted it and felt a pang of guilt. "So, what then?" he asked.

"Christian would pretend he owned us," Sally said. "He'd barter an hour or two of our company for a night's lodging and food. We'd go off with the men, Christian would loot the town or farm, wherever we happened to be, and then we'd run off."

"The men didn't chase you?" Glen asked.

"We mostly drugged them," Mia said. "Unless we particularly liked the look of one or two. The ones we didn't drug would be amused that they were the chosen ones, until after when we drugged them too."

"And if we couldn't drug them, we'd taze them," Sally said. "No one ever came after us. By the time they regained their senses we were long gone."

"Interesting way to make a living. Why switch MO and start killing people?" he asked.

"We ran out of roofies and couldn't find anymore. Tasers aren't easy to come by," Mia said.

"Besides, word got out and we got ambushed and had the crap beaten out of us. Christian said the only way to avoid that was to kill the people we stole from. But that meant we had to go after people without a community." Sally shrugged. "It's a dog eat dog world out there now."

Glen was shocked and it must've shown on his face because Sally turned and stomped from the kitchen. She sat on the coffee table close to Christian and wiped the tears from her face with her sleeve.

"And you're okay with this?" he asked Mia. "Killing people to stay alive doesn't diminish your humanity at all?"

"What does my humanity matter? "Mia retorted. "Kill or be killed, kill or be forced into sexual slavery, either way you lose your humanity. What would you know about it?"

"I know I've managed to stay alive without killing anyone," Glen said. "Surely that counts for something."

"Where were you when the lights went out?" she asked. "Not in the middle of Chicago, I can tell you that."

"No, but you could've left Chicago. You could have found yourself a place in Illinois to grow some food and raise some chickens, but instead you elected to rob people. And when that stopped working you elected to kill people. I did not. So, excuse me for thinking questions about your humanity are fair." He might have said more but Mia turned and crossed to where Sally was sitting.

She put her arm around Sally, who turned and buried her face in Mia's shoulder. They were rocking together when Glen slid out the door to the deck. He sat on the edge overlooking the pond and wondered what to do with these three.

They were clearly a threat, but he'd be jeopardizing his own humanity if he threw them out.

He couldn't access his food stores or his medical stores or leave them alone in the cabin. It was a problem. There wasn't much in the cupboard to eat without accessing the hidden stash. Yet, if they saw him do that, they would steal it. He had no doubt.

He caught a glimpse of bushy tail on the far side of the pond. "Go away," he whispered urgently. "It's not safe here now."

He had no proof that the three would harm the fox, but he had no proof that they wouldn't either. He would make an effort to leave some food for her away from the house in the hope she would stay away. He inwardly cursed himself. He had helped them and now he was responsible for them. He should have turned them away, humanity or no humanity.

He caught the sound of the door sliding, and a moment later Mia was sitting next to him.

"I hope you can forgive us," she said. "It's been a long time we felt safe anywhere. We had very little humanity left. If we hadn't found Christian, or rather if he hadn't found us, Sally probably would've killed herself. She's been badly mistreated by men."

"I can understand the need to protect yourself," Glen replied. "But killing? And not just killing because the circumstance demands it, but planning to kill? I hope I never get to that point."

"For your sake," Mia said, "I hope the same."

Glen stood up. "I need to get Christian a shot of penicillin," he said and went inside, leaving Mia on the deck.

Sally was curled up in a chair sleeping. He passed her quietly and slipped out the front door. He went to the truck and pulled out the medical kit he kept there, because he really couldn't get into his medical stores without one of them seeing him. He didn't want to lose his medical kit, but if they did decide to steal it, better this one.

In the bathroom he found what he needed, a syringe and needle, and he prepared the injection. Christian was unconscious and didn't even flinch as Glen shoved the needle into his thigh. He'd had to estimate the man's weight but was confident he'd gotten close enough.

He went to the kitchen and marked used on the packaging the needle had been in and reinserted it. Normal procedure would have been to dispose of the needle, but there wasn't an infinite supply, so he stored them in empty butter dish in the cupboard. He rinsed the syringe and did the same with it.

Then he pulled a surveyor's map of the local area out of the drawer and opened it onto the kitchen table. He smoothed the folds and use masking tape to hold it down. Three towns were within traveling distance, well, walking distance anyway. He wasn't about to fire up the truck for obvious reasons.

The closest town was out of bounds. He wouldn't even tell the three it existed. It was too close and it was possible he may need allies one day. The hardware store man might be willing to vouch for him, so he didn't even mark the town on the map.

The other two he circled. Then he marked the most direct route to each of them, using the contours on the map to help. He never walked over the top of hills, but skirted around them, unless he especially needed to get his bearings, or if he wanted to see what was going on down below. So, he marked the path in pencil, and then indicated a couple of high lookouts where they could scout the town below.

He was hoping they would agree to the farthest town. The farther away from his cabin the better. In fact, if Christian had been in better shape, he would've suggested a three-day march. But even waiting forty-eight hours, and taking it slowly, the two day march was going to be very hard on the wounded man. Christian needed a full course of antibiotics as soon as possible. If infection set in it could cause other complications and even his life.

CHAPTER SIX

MARGARET WAS LYING HALF-NAKED on a pile of hospital chucks covering a plastic sheet they had placed on the floor of his bedroom. Glen had offered her his bed, but she had refused, saying she didn't want to be responsible for ruining his mattress. She had refused the blankets and sheets for the same reason.

The medication he'd given her had worked, and she was expelling the unwanted pregnancy. But it wasn't easy. She cried with the physical pain, and possibly also the emotional pain of ending the life inside her. She shook first with cold, and then with fever. There was little Glen could do except remove the soiled chucks and give her sips of water.

He knew it happened that way sometimes, more like inducing labor than a woman's normal cycle, but he'd never witnessed it. Poor Brian was in the living room listening to his mother's cries of pain. Glen couldn't think of anything else to do with him. He didn't dare let them go out on the deck with the pond beckoning so close. Locking him in the truck would be cruel.

"I know it sounds bad," Glen said to the boy, "but your mom will be okay."

"What's happening?" Brian pleaded. "Why is my mom in pain?"

"I gave her some medicine," Glen said, "and it's making her stomach hurt." That at least was close to the truth. "Like when you have a bad tummy ache."

"Why did you give her that medicine?" the boy asked.

"She asked me to," Glen said truthfully. "It will make it easier for her to travel. She's trying to take you someplace safe."

"Is there someplace safe?" Brian looked at him with big eyes.

"I don't know, but if there is, your mom will find it. I have confidence in her." Glen wondered if this was true. He hadn't known Margaret long enough to really know, but it felt true to him. If she could find a safe place for her boy, she would. And she would continue looking.

An especially loud cry came from the other room and Glen went to check on Margaret.

"Sorry," she panted. "This is worse than labor. At least when you're giving birth you get a baby at the end of it." She smiled weakly. "I didn't know it was going to be this difficult."

"It isn't always, from what I understand," he said. "But medications affect people in different ways sometimes. The upside is I don't think you'll bleed for long. You're expelling everything now."

"Glad to know there is an upside," she said. "Because this is hell."

"I know and I'm sorry," he said. "I can give you some Tylenol, but I doubt it would cut the pain much."

"No, I lived through childbirth, I can live through this." She closed her eyes tight as another contraction racked her body. Then they popped open. "You don't have a hot water bottle, by any chance? Because that might actually help."

This search through the cabinets revealed that no, he did not have a hot water bottle. However, he had taken some towels from the cupboard and heated them on the wood stove, swapping them out as they became cold.

Margaret said that was helpful, so he continued until the contractions had lessened and she fell asleep. He covered her with a chuck, mostly so she wouldn't yell at him for ruining his things, and then covered her with his softest blanket.

"She's much better now," Glen told the boy. "Why don't you get some rest?"

Brian curled up on the couch and was asleep almost instantly. Glen covered him with a throw blanket he kept near the fire and sank into his armchair, exhausted himself. His head throbbed, and he couldn't shake the dizziness that had come with the concussion. He sank into sleep gratefully.

He woke to noises from the kitchen, where Margaret was preparing food.

"Should you be up?" he asked groggily.

"More than you should," she said. "You have a concussion, remember? You're supposed to take it easy."

Glen grunted. "Easier said than done around here," he said.

"It's probably not wise for me to travel while reeking of blood," she said. "So, if you don't mind, I'll stick around here for a day or two and take care of you until I stop bleeding. Sound fair?"

"More than fair," he said closing his eyes. "You already fixed my head. I wasn't asking for more than that." He felt himself beginning to drift again and didn't hear what she said in response.

When he woke again, there was a plate of stew on the table beside him. He poked his finger in, still warm. As he began eating he became aware of the sound of singing from outside on the deck. And then a child's laughter. He could almost imagine Sarah and Clarence out on the deck playing some childhood game. He pushed the thought away. Would it ever stop hurting to think of them?

He'd lost his appetite but forced himself to eat the stew. It was good. Margaret had been kind to make it for him, and he needed his strength. When he finished he was surprised to find he felt better, and the singing coming from the deck was pleasant instead of painful.

That night, they ate together, almost like a family, and Glen found himself enjoying Margaret's company. He entertained the thought of them staying. He could build a second bedroom for Brian, and if he fell again there'd be someone to come looking for him. To save him. When he realized he had imagined only a bedroom for Brian, he amended his fantasy, embarrassed. The second room could be for Margaret and Brian. He let the fantasy slip away, disconcerted that he'd created a new family for himself so easily just because she was there.

Add the singing woman and child, stir, and presto, instant family. He did not entertain that thought again.

But the days passed easily. Brian was fascinated by Glen's fox and spent hours on the deck, sitting quietly, waiting for her to show up. They ate most meals together, laughing and talking, and Margaret and Glen stayed up late chatting quietly at the kitchen table while Brian slept in Glen's bed.

Glen had given up his bed to Brian and Margaret, and was sleeping on the couch. Some part of him wished Brian was on the couch and he was sleeping with Margaret, but he wasn't ready to go there. He'd only get attached and then she'd leave.

He woke every morning to Margaret in the kitchen and Brian on the deck and life seemed happier than it had been in a long time. Margaret and Brian stayed longer than they needed, he knew that. And he knew she was staying because he was injured and she wanted to be sure he'd be okay. But the longer she stayed the more reliant on her he became, and the inevitable departure only became more painful.

One morning, he was sitting on the deck with Margaret while Brian fiddled at the edge of the pond. The boy was talking to himself and singing snatches of songs that he knew, perfectly happy in the sunshine.

"Will you stay?" Glen asked Margaret.

"Here with you, you mean?" she asked.

He nodded, watching her face. She was quiet for a few minutes, thinking it over, it seemed.

"No," she said. "If it were just me, then maybe I would. But I have Brian to think about. He needs a community. A place to belong to when he grows up. A place where people will care for him. If we stayed here, he will grow up alone, and then you and I would die maybe sooner than later. He would be all alone. No community, no companionship. No, I cannot stay. But you could come with us." She looked at him with her head tilted.

It was his turn to be quiet and think.

"No," he said. "I'm sorry, but I can't. I have a home here. I'm afraid if I left and went searching with you, that we wouldn't find the place you are searching for. What if there are no places with power? No community that would welcome us? We could walk for months or years, never having a place to rest. I would become impossible to live with. You would regret having asked me to come along. It's wouldn't be good."

He wondered, as he said it, if his words were true. Was it that he was afraid they'd never find civilization, or that they would, and he wouldn't fit in? Maybe he wasn't fit for society anymore. Maybe he couldn't make a home among people.

After all, he'd left before the world went dark. What made him think he could fit back in now?

So, he watched her pack up their belongings without telling her his real fears. He gave them a first aid kit, and some dried fruits and meat. He walked them to the road north and warned them to hide if they heard any noise, people or animals. Then he watched them walk away, and hoped, when they turned to wave goodbye, that they couldn't see his tears.

CHAPTER SEVEN

HIS THREE 'GUESTS,' he liked to think of them in quotes because they hadn't been invited, all were asleep the next morning when Glen got out of bed. He slipped quietly outside and decided to risk getting into the food cache. They needed something besides rice to eat.

But the moment he grabbed the line he heard a noise and quickly released it. He turned to see Sally in the doorway, rubbing her eyes.

"Morning," she said. "Do you have coffee?"

"I've been out of coffee for a year," he said. "I've got tea. I can offer you a combination of acorn and dandelion root, as a coffee substitute. The tea has caffeine, the other doesn't."

"Ugh, what I wouldn't give for fresh brewed coffee with real sugar and cream in it," Sally said. "I need caffeine, so I guess it's tea."

"Coming up," Glen said, and headed back inside. He turned as he entered the cabin and saw her looking into the pond where he had been standing. He'd have to be more careful, but luckily she'd have to be extremely clever to find the hidden lines to the cache. He had them well camouflaged.

He made 'coffee' and toasted some homemade soda bread while it brewed. Mia was moving and making waking-up noises as he took a tray out to Sally. He'd added some jam and honey to the tray for her bread and coffee, but he didn't have anything to substitute for cream.

Probably somebody somewhere nearby was raising dairy cows and bartering for milk, butter and cheese, but he didn't know who, and even if he did, contact with others was risking too much exposure. Milk products were not a necessity, only a nicety.

He left the tray and went to make toast for Mia, who had disappeared into the bathroom. He checked on Christian, noticing his color was good and his breathing even. But when he lifted the dressing to check the wound he was concerned. The lower end of the gash was angry red and swollen. Infection was setting in.

This complicated the situation greatly. He couldn't leave Christian here, because he'd likely return to find either Christian dead or himself robbed blind. Forcing Christian to travel put him at greater risk, but if he did travel he'd have antibiotics sooner. Glen didn't know if the penicillin really had expired, of if Christian was resistant to it, but it didn't matter. Either way, he needed something stronger, and soon.

He went out onto the deck, meaning to speak to the women, but as he watched them he realized they weren't women really. They were more than girls, certainly, but still very young. He wondered where their families were, and if they were searching for their children. He thought they might be in their early twenties, an age his own son never would reach. He had such an ache in his heart he thought he might die of it, but instead he would help these children. Maybe he could help them find their families.

First, he had to keep Christian alive.

"Mia, Sally," he called across the deck, "can I talk to you?"

They turned to him with worried faces, and he moved to join them. "Christian's wound is infected," he said. "I'll give him more antibiotics, but I'm afraid they aren't working on him. He may be resistant to penicillin. We need to find a town with a pharmacy."

"Isn't there some natural remedy you could try?" Sally asked. "Homeopathic or something like that?"

"I can make a poultice," he said. "But those are serious wounds, and the infection could spread. We need to do more than that."

"When can we leave?" Mia asked. "Couldn't I go and bring it back?"

"That's not a good idea," he began and Mia started to cut him off. "No. Listen," he said firmly. "First, as you have noticed, people aren't welcoming to strangers. You'd be vulnerable on your own." He could see she was about to interrupt again and lifted a hand to stop her. "Second, we need to get him medicine as fast as we can, and it still will be faster for us all to travel together, than to go all the way there and back again."

"But, I could move very quickly," Mia said. "I could be really fast."

"That's only if you got there and were able to negotiate for medicine quickly. I've got skills that may help us get what we need. We all need to go." He didn't add that she just as likely could be held captive or killed when she showed up, but it was true.

He went back in the house to concoct a combination of ginger, garlic, and honey. Then he spread it on a sterile dressing and laid it over the angry red area on Christian's stomach. He laid another sterile dressing over that, and administered another syringe of penicillin. He hated to waste it, but it might be helping a little. He sat back and thought about what materials he had at hand for placing a drain. He hoped it wouldn't come to that, but it might, so he'd better pack for that eventuality.

He left Christian and went to pull his pack from his bedroom closet. He had kept it ready, but double-checked for dried meat, bullets and other necessities. He added surgical supplies, but he didn't have any medical tubing. So, he grabbed a couple of plastic straws and higher-quality water bottles and hoped he wouldn't need to use them.

Then he packed two smaller backpacks with food and filled the water bottles he'd stolen the straws from. They still were somewhat usable. He also went out to the truck and pulled a trio of emergency blankets from behind the seat. He didn't have a fourth, but it wasn't so cold yet that he'd need to bring a sleeping bag. He'd survive in his jacket. He split the foil blankets between the three packs, zipped them up and placed them by the door. They were ready to leave as soon as Christian was mobile.

Christian regained consciousness later that afternoon. Sally and Mia were playing cards, a crazy version of war, Glen thought, while he pondered ways of moving Christian. If the man wasn't ready by the next day, they would have to transport him. Perhaps they could create a litter from the wheel barrow and chance traveling down the road.

Then Christian raised his head and said, "Why do I smell of garlic? It's making me hungry," which Glen took as a good sign.

The girls dropped the cards and rushed to Christian's side, making an extraordinary amount of racket.

"I'm fine. I'm fine," he said. "Who do you have to, uh, ask to get some food around here?"

Sally jumped up to dish him up a bowl of rice and Glen joined her.

"Not too much to begin with," he said. "We don't want

him vomiting at this stage of his healing. He could split his stitches."

Sally dumped half the rice back in the pot, and poured a glass of room temperature water before bringing them both to Christian.

Christian accepted them with thanks, and Glen cautioned him to go easy.

So, Christian ate at a moderate speed while Mia spelled out the situation. Having finished, Christian handed the bowl back to Sally. "So, when do we leave?" he asked. "Soon, I hope." He touched the bandage over his belly. "Wouldn't want to die of septicemia."

"No, you wouldn't," Glen agreed. "So, we will leave tomorrow. It's a two-day journey and I doubt we'll be able to travel very quickly. We will stick together, even though Mia has offered to go ahead, because there is safety in numbers, and also because if you have a relapse, Christian, it will take all three of us to keep you moving. How is your stomach feeling after eating?"

"I'm not feeling like I'm going to upchuck, if that's what you mean, but I still smell really sweet garlic." Christian sniffed loudly. "I think it's coming from me."

"It's a poultice of garlic honey and ginger," Glen said. "They have antibiotic properties. But let me take a look at how you are doing."

He gently released the outer bandage, which was stained not only with honey, but also, Glen thought, with pus. "Sally," he said, "can you go into the bathroom and get me some more sterile pads? I'm going to need to change this."

Sally looked mulish, "Why don't you ever ask Mia to fetch sterile pads?" she asked.

"Because you know where they are so you're quicker," he said, barely keeping his patience. "And I ask her to do other things."

"I suppose," she muttered and got up to do as he asked.

Glen pulled off the poultice and wiped the honey mixture from Christian's skin with the nearly clean outer bandage. The infection hadn't abated, but didn't look as though it had gotten any worse either. Sally returned with the supplies, and Glen put more honey mixture on the sterile gauze and bandaged Christian back up.

"There you are," Glen said. "We'll leave that until morning. I'll change it again before we leave."

"Thanks, Doc," Christian said. "Don't suppose I could get a shot of whiskey for the pain?"

"Uh, no." Glen gave Christian his best disapproving look. "Not happening. You can have a non-narcotic painkiller if you like."

Christian looked disappointed. "I suppose that will have to do. Meanwhile, I need to use the loo. If I'm walking tomorrow, I probably should try standing today."

"That would be a good idea," Glen said, "but let me help you."

"I'll help him," Mia said.

"It may take two of us to get him standing," Glen said. He placed his arm behind Christian's shoulders so he could achieve a sitting position without straining his stitched muscles. Mia helped him to swing his legs off the couch and together they got him upright. He seemed pretty steady on his feet so Glen let Mia walk with him into the bathroom.

There was giggling on the other side of the door, and Glen thought Christian must be feeling better than he'd thought possible if he could laugh while Mia was helping him urinate. Then the door opened and the pair returned to the living room, Christian hardly putting any weight on Mia at all. Sally came in from the deck and grinned like a fool when she saw Christian standing.

This was good, Glen thought. They were in better spirits

and Christian looked strong. They just needed to keep him that way.

"See if you can walk around on your own" he said to Christian. "Mia, take him out to the deck for a stroll around the pond."

Glen watched the three of them meander around the pond. They were in good spirits and Christian seemed to be moving well, but Glen had his doubts about the trek. It was a long way and, as chipper as Christian seemed now, he had a severe injury. Maybe he should pull out the truck. They could drive there in a couple of hours and be back in a day.

But Sarah was in his head, telling him to take care of himself. Don't waste the gas, don't risk losing the truck. There might come a time you'll need it. If you walk the three to the far town, there will be no reason for them to come back here. You'll be safe. But the guilt tugged on him as well, telling him he was being selfish. He found himself walking out to the truck, keys in hand.

He was saved from himself. The truck had two flat tires. When had that happened? Were they flat when he came out to get the first aid kit? He didn't think so. Which meant those women still were considering carrying out their initial plan. They let the air out of the tires so he couldn't drive away.

He walked back into the house, returned the truck keys to the hook and went to stand by the window overlooking the deck. They still were out there goofing around. Acting like the children they were. Deadly children. Who knew what was going on in their heads? He'd have to be careful. He wanted to come back in one piece. As far as he knew, they could be planning to kill him and take his cabin. Probably after he'd gotten them the medical supplies they needed.

He'd better make sure they couldn't figure out the way back. And he'd better be sure they couldn't get to him without first waking him up. He went back to his closet and pulled out his bivy, a small tent just big enough for one person. He also grabbed his Ferro rod for starting fires and some duct tape.

He dropped those items in his bug-out bag and went into the kitchen. The stovetop and oven were propane-powered. Hopefully, there was enough fuel left to bake some traveling bread. It was a recipe he'd created for days he was out hunting. It was high in protein, traveled well, and stayed good to eat for days. They'd get tired of eating it, but they'd also be grateful to have it.

He was kneading dough when the trio came back inside. Christian was worn out and headed back to the couch with Mia by his side, but Sally came to see what Glen was doing. She took a slab of the dough and worked companionably beside him, following his lead. They created forty-eight discs of dough and placed them in the oven to rise.

When they'd first arrived he'd thought of Sally as spineless and weak, but maybe that wasn't the case. She had a sense of calm around her now. She listened well and paid attention. There was a kind of quiet confidence about her.

"I'm going to sit on the deck while that rises," he said to her. "Want to come?"

"Sure," she said, glancing over at Christina and Mia, who both were sound asleep on the couch and chair. "Anyway, we won't wake them if we're outside."

"What did you do in the real world, before this all happened?" Glen asked Sally. "Before the lights went out, I mean."

"I knew what you meant," she said. "I was a photography student. I took wedding photos and pictures of kids and dogs to pay the bills, but I wanted to be a photojournalist. I don't think anyone does that anymore? Do you? It's not like you could sell photos online anymore, even if money had any value."

"I suppose not," he said. "Do you still own a camera?"

"No. I don't own much of anything. We stashed our backpacks before Christian was attacked by the bear and I'm not sure we could even find them again. There wasn't much in them because we'd traded the good stuff for food. What about you? Where you when it all ended?"

"I was here," he said. "I left my old life behind some years before it happened." It seemed a long time ago now, but Sarah still was ever present in his head. He wondered why that was. Maybe because he'd been isolated.

"What did you do before you came here?" she asked.

"I was a doctor," he said. "I lived in Philadelphia."

"What kind of doctor were you? Like a primary care physician?" She looked at him sideways. "No not a primary care doc, some kind of specialist. Like maybe a..."

"A neurosurgeon," he said. "Not primary care."

She laughed. "See? I was right. A specialist. Was the job too stressful? Is that why you came here?"

A breeze blew across the pond, rippling the water and lifting the hair around Sally's face. He thought about lying, not telling her the story, but why? What was the point in keeping it a secret now?

"I was in a car accident," he said. "It killed my wife and child but I survived. When I recovered I didn't want to practice medicine anymore. I couldn't."

"Did you lose your muscle dexterity in your fingers?" she asked.

"No. There just didn't seem to be any point without my family. Without them I just didn't care anymore. So, you have a brain tumor or hydrocephalus, maybe some weird genetic anomaly, so what? At least you are alive." He paused. "There are hundreds of great brain doctors out there. No one is missing me."

She was silent for a few minutes and Glen's thoughts began focusing on tomorrow's journey. So, he was taken aback when she spoke.

"I'm sorry about your family," she said quietly. "That must have been horrible." She shook her head slowly. "To be the only one left alive." She trailed off. "Did you feel guilty? Did guilt drive you out here?" She put a hand to her mouth. "I'm sorry. That was tactless. You don't have to answer."

Glen gave her a sad smile. "The sorrow more than the guilt," he said. "I had a huge hole inside me and it was such an effort to have to speak to people with the best parts of me missing. I just couldn't take it. I actually didn't think I'd make it this long. I figured I was coming here to die. I just didn't."

"You lived despite yourself," Sally said.

"Something like that." He stretched and got up. "Time to take out the travel bread from the oven," he said. "And then double-check my supplies for our trip. Are you coming in?"

"No. I think I'll sit out here for a bit." She smiled up at him. "I'll be in later."

CHAPTER EIGHT

GLEN WAS PULLING the bread from the oven when Sally came flying in, her face alight. "There's a fox out there," she said excitedly. "Did you know you have a fox? She just stood and looked at me for the longest time."

"She was hoping for some food," Glen said. "She's the closest I've ever come to having a dog. Only better because she can take care of herself if something happens to me. She saved my life once."

"How did a wild fox save your life?" Mia asked from the chair across the room.

"I fell off a cliff and she wouldn't stop yipping at me. I might have just gone to sleep and never woken up, but she made so much noise that I finally had to get up and rescue myself." He smiled. The memory was not as horrifying as it once had been.

"Wow," Sally said. "That's wild and ridiculously cool. Not everyone can say they have a fox as a companion."

"I guess not," Glen said, putting the last tray of rolls on the counter to cool. "Her kits are usually friendly too, but they don't stick around. Sometimes I think I see one when

I'm roaming around or hunting, but it's hard to tell. One fox looks very much like another."

Mia got up from her chair. "Is it still out there?" she asked. "I want to see it."

"I think it went back to its den," Sally said. "It kind of flicked its tail at me and disappeared into the long grass."

"She'll have gone to hunt," Glen said. "I don't think she'll come back here tonight. Come and have some food while it's warm." He pulled a potato pie he'd made while the bread was cooking from the oven. "Carbs for our trip tomorrow."

Christian woke and joined them at the table, although he didn't eat much. Glen would have to check that wound again tonight. But for now he turned his attention to Mia.

"What did you do in the real world, before the power went out, Mia?" he asked.

"I went to school with Sally," she said, through a mouthful of potatoes. "Studied something irrelevant. Oh yeah, classical languages. Whole lot of good that will do me now. Should have studied forestry or something useful like that. Did they have classes in survival, Sal? We should have taken those."

"I doubt it," Sally said, "and even if they did, you would have skipped them. Learning was not your objective at college."

"What was your objective?" Glen asked.

"Finding a suitable husband," Mia said. "At least according to my mother. She didn't care a fig about what I studied or if I passed classes as long as I could live at college and try finding a good man. I mean, really. What if I'd been gay? Would I have been looking for a good woman?"

"Your mother would have passed out cold if you'd brought a woman home." Sally was laughing so hard she hardly could get the words out. "Can you imagine her face?"

Mia's face fell and Glen thought she was fighting back tears.

"I can't really see her face anymore," she said, and her chin quivered.

"Oh God, I'm sorry, Mia. I wasn't thinking." Sally looked stricken.

"Come on, Mia, let's go look at the stars," Christian said, and stood up. Mia followed him outside.

"Mia's family was rich," Sally explained, "and after the lights went out looters came to her house and killed her family. She hid in a cupboard in the laundry room and when she came out everyone was dead. They'd slashed her mom's face to pieces. It was horrific."

"How brutal for her," Glen said, "and it explains a lot."

"Like what?" Sally asked.

"Her fierceness when you first came here. Also, her attachment to a large Latino man with tattoos covering his arms. Who, by the way, is far too old for her. It's hard to see anyone taking Christian by surprise." Which was another reason Glen would have to be very careful.

"I see how you could think that, but I'm not sure you're right. She's always been attracted to bad boys in motorcycle leathers and tattoos." Sally wrinkled her nose. "Sort of, anyway. I think mostly they were wannabes."

"Mia went out with motorcycle gang wannabes?" Glen said. "Really? I thought she was more perceptive than that."

"There aren't many actual bonafide Hells Angels on university campuses, you know. They tend to have their degrees already, legit jobs, and tons of money. I think she was stuck with the not-so bad boys." Sally shrugged. "Not that her parents knew the difference, so it was a win-win for Mia."

"I can see that," Glen said, suddenly glad he didn't have a daughter with the need to rebel. "So now she has her bonafide bad boy. Too bad the world had to end for her to get it. I mean him."

"It is probably more PC these days," Sally said. "Anyway, I

knew what you meant." She rested her elbows on the table and cupped her chin in her hands.

"That's the trouble with growing up with money. It's so much harder to figure out who you are. And then there is all the rebelling against Daddy's money." She sighed. "It's taken Mia quite a while to really come into her own. And truthfully, I don't think she's there yet. Now she's got arrested development from being in the house when her family was killed. They killed the servants too. It was brutal. So unnecessary. And what's that stuff really going to get them in this world? Not much, I don't think."

"Probably not," Glen said, thinking that Sally had talked more in the last ten minutes than all the time before that since they'd arrived at his door. And he wondered why. What had changed that made her want to talk? He shrugged. What did it matter, really?

"It's a long day tomorrow," he said. "Best head to sleep." He got up and went to the door, cracked it open, and called out into the night. "Don't stay out too late," he said. "We've got a lot of walking to do tomorrow." Then he slid the door closed. "Good night," he said to Sally, and headed down the hall to his room.

"Good night," he heard her call after him. He wondered if she was a little forlorn.

He'd hoped that he would drop right off to sleep, but his mind wouldn't quiet. There was so much that could go wrong over the next couple of days. Even in normal times a two-day hike took some preparation and he would have thought twice about bringing a trio of untried newbies.

He rolled over and bunched his pillow under his head. He tried deep breathing, but his eyes kept popping open. It was the same thing that used to happen to him when he became a surgeon. The beginning of his career was a litany of sleepless nights reviewing every detail of the upcoming surgery. So, instead of fighting it, he let his mind wander over the activities of the day to come.

He would take them out by the road. Because they didn't already know the back roads, and he didn't really know which way they came in. So, they'd go out by the road, and go the opposite way of the town, which just happened to be the most direct route. Although taking the direct route was not the most important thing here. He could hear Sarah's voice in his ear. Don't worry about them, worry about you. She used to say, "The administration can take care of itself. You do what you need to for the patient and yourself. Everyone else can look after their own business."

He found himself missing her. She was always on his side. The perfect wife. He gave himself a minute to feel the sadness and regret, then shook his head. Back to business: how to stay alive and get back here in one piece.

So, they'd take the road for maybe five hours, ducking off it if they heard signs of people. It was possible they'd come across roadblocks, or maybe an ambush. So, they'd have to be vigilant and he also would have to carry a weapon. He wondered if he should arm the others, but decided against it. It was too easy to fall prey to his own firearm.

So, five hours down the road and then cut into the wilderness. Skirt Black Mountain, which really was more of a hill, cross the river above Black Falls, and camp on the far side. There they would have water and the falls would muffle any noise they might make. If there was enough mist coming off the water, they could have a small fire, and dry anyone who'd gotten wet in the crossing. Depending on the water level they might be able to get across dry, but he doubted it. One misstep on a slippery rock and in the water you went.

The following day they would head upstream and then circle east, coming at the town from the far side, further protecting the location of his home base. He felt a twinge of guilt. They could reach the town in one day if they started out through the woods and went directly there. But that he would not do. Sarah would not approve.

The route east from the falls had its own set of problems. There was a ravine to cross. There used to be a rope bridge that the community had erected for local hunters, but it could be guarded, or gone. So, they'd have to play that one by ear. The ravine could be traversed in a couple of different places, it just was a matter of finding them and making sure they weren't guarded.

There was a ridge to the north of the town that made a good outlook, but the downfall was the track to the town was narrow and easily guarded. The alternative route was a circuitous one that added hours to the trek and skirted a number of old farms that still could be inhabited. So, he'd hope for the shorter track, but they'd just have to see. It was possible they'd get to the ridge and then have to spend another entire day getting to the town.

He hoped Christian would hold up to the stresses. They really didn't need for him to succumb to an infection and be unable to travel. Which reminded him, he'd need to double-check the first aid kit. He needed to be able to repair that wound if it ripped or started to seep. And there was always the chance that one of the others would get hurt.

And then a thought struck him. Was it possible that Christian had tangled with a bear on purpose so Glen would open the door to him? Was it worth it to Christian to be wounded to get his foot in Glen's door? And was it his stuff that they wanted, or his help in gaining access to the town?

A cold shiver ran down his back. Was this the trap? To take him to the town and use him to gain access? Or to trade him for a spot in the community, or safe passage? A surgeon would be a valuable asset, especially if they had a need for a doctor. Was he walking into a trap? Very possibly. So, he'd have to pay attention and watch them.

He briefly thought about ditching them someplace, the falls perhaps. But he decided against it. What if they hadn't planned the bear attack? Christian really needed help and Glen was fairly certain he could talk himself out of any situation where his life or freedom was at risk. Every community needed a doctor, and he had more specialized skills than any he'd heard of around here. He could keep himself alive and plan an escape if needed. He just hoped it wasn't needed.

CHAPTER NINE

CHRISTIAN'S WOUND was almost unchanged the next morning, which was disappointing considering Glen had given him another shot of penicillin before dinner the night before. But despite the creeping red gash, he had plenty of energy and was up early and ready to go.

Glen distributed the travel bread between the four of them. You could eat what you carried when you felt you needed it, and no one was appointed to the rationing police. Same with the water. Although, truth be told, there were plenty of rivers, lakes and streams in this part of Michigan and Glen had water purification tablets. They didn't have to carry more than a couple of hours worth each.

They had arrived on his doorstep with nothing in their hands, so Glen gave each of them a small day pack to carry their food, water and space blanket. Glen's own pack was much bigger, as he was carrying all the survival supplies. He was not tempted to divvy those heavier items out to the others. For one thing, he was used to carrying the weight while hunting. For another, they'd be less tempted to try stealing the bag if they had to kill him first.

He secretly was hoping that once they reached the town, the three would say goodbye and approach it on their own. He'd seen what these communities were like, and he didn't relish the idea of having dealings with them. He'd love to just fade back into the wilderness and take the fast way home.

He left one last meal for the fox family before they headed out, hoping for a last glimpse of her, but she didn't come. He left the food near the pond and locked the back door before meeting the others around the front. He left the front unlocked. Unless he was willing to board up all the windows anyone with determination would be able to get in anyway. May as well save himself the trouble of fixing a broken door or window.

They headed down the driveway, and when they reached the road Glen saw the barrier had been partially torn down. They took a few minutes to rebuild the blind that helped block the driveway, although it was pretty well grown over by now. Still, if Christian and the girls could find it, others could too.

He walked into the brush near the driveway to grab a live branch for the finishing touch and Glen saw a tarp thrown over what looked like a rock. He picked up the edge and found three backpacks, a shotgun and a shovel hidden underneath. Not that it was a surprise. Sally had said that they'd stashed their gear. The question was should he confront them and make them take their gear with them, or leave it be and hope they didn't attempt to come back for it?

He was contemplating this when Mia came crashing through the undergrowth.

"What's taking so long, Glen?" She stopped when she saw what he was looking at.

"Maybe you should take your belongings," he said. "It would be better if you didn't have to try finding your way here again." He was angry, and bitter, but he tried keeping his voice even. "Maybe you could pass on killing me this time, in payment for stitching up Christian?"

"You were right, Chris," she yelled. "He found our stuff."

Glen went back to finding a good branch to finish off the blind. There was a thin maple with a branch of leaves that had begun changing color. That should serve until he returned. He left the others gathering their gear and went back to the road. When he'd finished the drive camouflage he stood in the middle of the main road and waited. There were no sounds that might indicate human presence, except for the murmuring of his group.

He assumed they were discussing how to proceed, and he hoped it didn't include a plan where he was held at gunpoint. If they tried that tactic, he'd lead them deep into the bush and push them over a cliff. He was just that fed up with the three of them. Here he was trying to help them, and they were in there debating when to kill him. Or at least that's what he assumed.

He considered taking off at a run in the opposite direction. He might make it to his "home" town before they were able to shoot him. If he ran through the bush and not up the road anyway. But while he was trying to decide if that was a good idea, they appeared on the side of the road, Sally holding the gun barrel down, in a non-threatening manner.

She brought the gun and handed it to him. "We thought you'd be more comfortable if you carried the weapon," she said.

"We know that you know that we came here ready to kill you. But you saved Christian's life and have treated us so well." She paused and blushed. "We've decided it would not be right to kill you. And anyway, you don't really have anything that would help us in our travels. So, if you still are willing to show us the town, so we can get supplies and medicine, we'd be grateful."

Christian and Mia remained standing at the edge of the road with what Glen could have sworn were looks of hopeful anticipation on their faces. He wondered if they'd practiced them in the mirror. Very uncharitable, he chided himself.

"We'd better get moving," he said. "We've wasted enough time here." He shouldered the shotgun and wondered how many handguns they were carrying in their bags. He'd just have to count on the fact that they did not know where they were going and needed him to keep them from getting lost in the wilderness. He was surprised to find he wasn't ready to die yet. Not ready to join his wife and child in the afterlife. That was a new development.

He was relieved when Christian and the girls decided to walk in front of him. It meant he didn't have to focus his attention to the rear and could keep his attention on what was ahead. A couple of times he made them detour into the woods for a while when he'd seen or hear something up ahead. If his instincts gave him prickles up the back of his neck, he directed them off the road. He wasn't taking any chances.

The air was cool, but not cold, and the sun was warm, but not too hot. It was the kind of crisp late summer weather that Glen had loved as a young man. A perfect day for hiking, although perhaps what they were doing now was more like a forced march. The others were quiet and Glen wasn't sure if that was why. It was hard to tell what they were feeling, and if it had anything to do with Glen's discovery of their stash. Sally had lied to him when she'd said they'd dumped their bags, when they were purposefully stashed.

And what about that wound of Christian's? They said it was a bear, but what if he convinced one of the girls to slash him? What kind of man faked a bear attack to gain access to someone's home? Or could they have had an argument and one of the girls lashed out? The timing of the thing bothered him, as did Christian's state of mind. He would need to keep his eyes open.

When the sun was overhead they stopped to eat and rest. Glen chewed his roll slowly. Travel bread really was best when it had become a little stale and was chewy. While it still was soft, like it was now, it was too easy to wolf it down and eat too much. So, he paced himself and sipped water between every bite. He wanted to feel full, but not bloated or sloshy.

Mia went off into the bushes and came back stomping mad a few minutes later. "I swear," she said, "female biology is just limiting. Like I need to be able to conceive babies." She turned to Glen. "Would you give a woman a hysterectomy if she wanted it? It's not like you can just go to a freaking drug store and get your monthly supplies or anything."

"I'd advise the use of birth control pills," he said. "A hysterectomy, under these conditions, could be dangerous."

"So, yeah, birth control stops conception, but doesn't do a damn thing about the monthly," she practically spat out.

"You misunderstand me," Glen said. "If you take them every day, and don't skip a week each month, your body will react like it's pregnant and you won't have a monthly period. I'm sure there's probably a good supply of birth control pills in the world. I suggest bartering for some of those."

"As if," Sally said. "We've basically reverted to a rule by might scenario – patriarchy. Which means all women's issues are held hostage. I wish I'd grown up doing some kind of martial arts and shooting firearms."

"We could start a band of women," Mia joined in, "who roam the country freeing women from idiot macho men and forcing them to behave or else. The men, I mean, not the women we'd free."

"That's all well and good," Christian said dryly, "but you didn't and you can't. And meanwhile, back in the real world, I need antibiotics. So, maybe we should get a move on."

Mia shot Sally a look and Sally rolled her eyes. Glen thought if these women were ever in charge, Christian had better watch out. He might be the first to go.

"From here we leave the road," Glen said. "Watch where you walk. If you sprain your ankle, we only have two options – wrap it tight and you continue walking, or we leave you behind."

Sally rolled her eyes at him and he could almost hear her thinking 'Duh!' He cracked his neck once on the right and once on the left, which made her wince, and then they headed out.

The going was a lot slower off the road. Glen knew where the game trails were, but it would take a while to reach them. Besides that, a game trail was not a paved road. There would be a path, but it still would be rough going. He watched them picking their way through the undergrowth and was satisfied that all three were being extra careful.

The odd thing about being in the back was that he had to call out directions so the others knew where to go. He also felt stupid being in the back with the gun, he would be the last one to come across something that needed shooting. Yet, he wasn't about to give up the tactical advantage of being in the back when it came to his group. They weren't trustworthy and he knew it.

At one point he almost ran into the other three, who were stopped dead in their tracks. They'd reached the game trail and there in the middle of it was a fox. It stood over a dead rabbit with stiff legs, watching them with his ears flat, and lip curled back. You wouldn't think a fox could look so menacing, but even a small dog had a nasty bite. And this guy was a lot bigger than a small dog.

"It's okay, boy," Glen said. He was hoping this was one of his foxes and maybe it would remember his voice. "We don't want your rabbit. We are going to back away slowly, and you can take it back to your den. Okay?" This last part was for the others, of course, so they'd know what to do.

He took several steps backward without turning around, and the others did the same. It took longer than Glen anticipated to move out of the fox's danger zone, but when they finally did, the fox grabbed the rabbit, turned and disappeared back down the trail. Glen let his breath out.

"He's gone," he said and, surprisingly, his voice sounded steady. "Let's get going. We need to cross the river before nightfall."

It was an hour of steady walking before Glen began hearing the falls, and another thirty minutes after that before they came into view. Glen was surprised by the amount of water spilling over them. He thought by this time the flow would have abated, but the river was very full. They would have to be careful crossing at the fjord.

The climb to the top of the falls was grueling. Even Glen, who was pretty fit, was winded when he reached the top. They sat on the bank catching their breath, but not trying to talk. The roar of the falls made verbal communication useless.

When Glen felt he'd waited long enough for Christian to have recovered, he pulled a thin but very strong rope from his pack. He took it to a tree near the crossing place and tied it to the trunk. He eyed his little band of wannabe tough guys and motioned them to stay put. They looked pretty much done in. But he wanted to cross the river today, when they still had time to dry off and rest before moving on. So, he wrapped the rope around his waist and waded into the river.

The string of boulders that he normally used to cross the river was completely submerged and when he stepped onto the first rock, the pull of the current was strong. He moved slowly. The water wicked up his pant legs, making them heavy. On top of that, the water was ice-cold and he was going to lose coordination pretty quickly. But he let out the rope a little at a time and moved slowly and deliberately.

At the mid-point, the spot that was tricky even when the rocks stood above the water, he slipped and fell into the deep water. He had anticipated this, and kept his head, doling out the rope as he let the water push him downstream until he came up against a rock. From there he was able push toward the far shore, where he crawled out and lay on the bank for a few minutes.

For a moment he thought about not getting up. Just untying the rope and leaving the others to fend for themselves. But he'd be condemning them to die, most likely. So, he got up, found a second tree and pulled the rope tight across the river. Then he hooked a carabiner to the rope and a pant loop and made his way back across the river for the others.

They were at the shore near the tree, and the girls looked scared when he came back out of the water. He could see their mouths moving, but he couldn't hear a thing. So, he just smiled and gestured in a way that he hoped conveyed that he needed to sit down for a few minutes. He gave himself ten minutes with his eyes closed. If they wanted to kill him, they could just have at it.

CHAPTER TEN

HE DID FINALLY GET them all over to the other side, but it was a near-death thing with Christian. If Glen hadn't attached him to the line, Christian would have gone over the falls for certain. The two of them made it about a third of the way across, Glen in front showing him the way, when Christian lost his footing and went under.

Glen grabbed hold of his arm, but Christian must have been caught in an eddy because he was having trouble getting back on his feet. They struggled for a few minutes, Glen hauling him up, but Christian not being able to stand, until Glen finally realized they both were going to drown if he didn't change tactics. So, he changed his grip, grabbing the floundering Christian under his arms and hauling him across the river to the bank.

It took a minute to get him up on the bank, and when he did, Glen saw that the front of Christian's shirt was covered in blood. His medical supplies were in his pack on the far side of the river and he was exhausted. "Damn it," he muttered under his breath – not that anyone could have heard him. He made Christian lie on the ground, and he pulled up his shirt.

It wasn't as bad as it could have been. The lower end of the wound had ripped open, but at least it wasn't the entire length of it. Hopefully, the river was clean. Because who knew what could get in there and infect him.

"Put pressure on that," he yelled at Christian, but it was clear from the look on his face, he couldn't hear.

He grabbed Christian's hand, bunched his shirt in it, and pressed it to the wound. Christian nodded and held it there.

Glen headed back to the other side of the river. He grabbed his pack and the rifle, motioned to the girls to stay put, and made his way back across with the pack balanced on his head and the gun stock held horizontal, resting on his shoulder. He got to the other side, opened the pack and pulled out the medical kit. He used a hospital chuck to dry the area around the wound after wringing out the bottom edge of Christian's shirt. He needed the area to stay dry.

Then Glen removed his own long sleeve button down shirt and the T-shirt underneath so he wouldn't drip in Christian's wound and used the chuck to dry his head, chest, hands and arms. When he was as dry as possible he set out the items he'd need.

There wasn't anything to dull the pain, so he warned the injured man the best he could, and started stitching with a pre-threaded needle from the medkit. Christian's reaction was instantaneous. He balled his fists and Glen thought at first he was going to smash him in the face. But he clenched his entire body and stayed absolutely rigid – until he passed out.

Glen was worried. The stitches shouldn't have been that painful, especially as the cold river should have numbed him somewhat, but he was also grateful. It was much easier to work on an unconscious person. He could pull the stitches quickly, get done and get a fire going to warm Christian back

up again. As he knotted the last stitch, he looked across the
river to see how the women were fairing.

They weren't there.

He was amazed to see them mid-river, both attached to
the line running across the river by a rope around their waist.
They had stripped down to bra and panties. Neither was
carrying anything, which confused him, but then he saw that
they were dragging a length of rope behind them. And they
had attached a second rope high in the tree he'd used to
secure the rope.

"Now what are you up to?" he asked out loud, but seeing
that they were doing okay, he starting collecting wood for a
fire. He kept an eye in their direction, but they had the team-
work down. One would brace herself before the other moved.
They worked their way across the river as a team.

He pulled his Ferro rod from his pack and was starting
the fire as they climbed up onto the bank. But rather than
come warm themselves up, they moved to the tree that held
the other end of his rope. Mia jumped, caught a branch, and
hauled herself up. When she was high enough she motioned
to Sally to throw her the line, and when Sally did, Mia caught
it and wound it tightly around the branch. Then, with Sally
bracing her body against the tree to keep the line tight, Mia
pulled the backpacks across the line, high enough above the
river that the bags didn't touch the water.

Glen dragged Christian closer to the fire, so he could dry
out. When he looked up the women were there with the
backpacks. They had dressed in dry clothes and looked
perfectly comfortable, which made Glen irritable. Why
hadn't he thought to keep his clothes dry?

They stripped a half-conscious Christian down to his
boxers and laid his clothes on rocks near the fire to dry. Mia
dug through a backpack and came up with a pair of sweatpants and a long sleeve knit shirt. Then she yanked Christ-

ian's soaking boxers off him and Glen helped her pull the sweatpants on. They did the same with his shirts.

Glen pulled his bivy out of his pack and popped it open. It was a tiny tent, just big enough for him to lie in, but it would give him some privacy. He too had a set of dry clothes in his bag, but unlike Christian, he had the ability to change on his own.

When Glen was dry and in clean clothes, he checked Christian's bandages and saw that the wound had begun to weep pus. No wonder Christian had had trouble keeping his feet in the river, his body was fighting infection. Glen felt the twinge of guilt for making the three travel farther than necessary. They could have been at the town about now had they travelled directly.

He pushed the guilt aside. There was nothing he could do about that now, and he had every right to protect himself. They'd said themselves they were out to kill.

Because they couldn't communicate over the noise of the falls there wasn't much to do but eat, relax by the fire, and go to sleep. Before they all dropped off he motioned to the women to help him slide Christian into the bivy. That way if there was rain or a heavy dew the man wouldn't get wet again.

Christian struggled to help, but in the end it was just easier for him to lie still while Glen took his shoulders and the women each took a leg and moved him into the tent. Then they each found a spot not far from the fire to bed down. Glen slept with his hand on the rifle, just in case.

The next day was slow going. Christian was able to get up and move around, but he was slow and clumsy. Glen was positive he was running a fever, but there wasn't much he could do about it besides give him over the counter pain relievers.

By the time they had broken camp it was late morning, and Glen kept the pace slow. It would take most of the day to get there at this pace, but it was that or carry Christian. And he really didn't want to carry Christian.

They stopped to rest every hour, and each time Christian was slower to recover. When they broke for lunch, he didn't want to eat.

"Just let me sleep for a while," he said to Glen. "I'm not hungry."

But Glen made him eat half a travel bread before he'd let him sleep. "Your body needs fuel," he said. "Eat and then sleep."

It was late afternoon when they reached the cliff overlooking the town. They set up the bivy, hidden by bushes, and left Christian to sleep. Then the three of them crawled to the edge of the cliff to look down over the town. Mia and Sally sucked in their breath, and even Glen was surprised. The town looked like a war zone.

About a mile from town, to the north, a fuel tanker was flipped onto its side, blocking the road. Glen couldn't see that far to the south, but he'd put money on there being a similar roadblock down there. There were cinder block walls built across the smaller roads. It was as if someone had stood in the center of town and decided to build a wall across every road seven blocks from the center. Glen wondered what the people who lived eight blocks out thought of this plan. Not that there were many houses past that point, it was a pretty small town.

Beyond the walls, cars had been abandoned in the streets. In fact, as Glen examined the town below him, he realized that while there were a few old trucks and station wagons in the town, all the newer vehicles, those that would have been rendered useless by the Space Storm, had been pushed out of the center of town. The older cars and trucks were apparently still useful, and they were parked around the town green.

"Didn't you say you had binoculars?" Sally asked. "Why not get them out?"

"Because the sun might catch the lenses and give us away," Glen said. "We can use them in the morning, or at dusk, but right now... I don't think so."

"Smart," Mia muttered under her breath, and Glen wondered if they'd been trying to trick him. But that didn't make any sense. If he got caught, they got caught.

He went back to his examination of the town. Two ways in and two ways out, at least by vehicle. On foot it might be easier.

"I'm not getting a good feeling about this place," Glen said. "They don't look like they welcome strangers."

"Tell me something I don't already know," Sally said. "That place is a fortress."

"Yeah," Mia added, "I don't think we are just going to walk up and get let in."

"Exactly," Glen said. "I think we are going to have to sneak in and steal what we need."

"That seems kind of risky," Sally said. "Couldn't we at least try asking for help first?"

"We could, but if we do, they are going to be watching out for us," Glen said. "If we sneak in and out without them knowing we are here, they don't have time to prepare for us. If you get my meaning."

"I don't know," Sally said. "I still think we should at least try."

"Before we do anything," Mia said, "I think we need to get a closer look."

Glen nodded. "My thoughts exactly. See down there?" he said, pointing to an area right below them. "That line of fence behind that row of houses?"

"I see it," Mia said, and Sally nodded.

"It seems like there might be a break in the fence, or

possibly a gate." Glen rubbed his forehead with the ball of his thumb. "If we could get through there, we could sneak between two houses and then into the town. I'm suggesting we go down and circle the town and see what we can see from the woods. Stay under cover of the trees for now and see what the lay of the land looks like. If we split up, take thirds, we could check it out and be back up here before sunset. Are you willing?"

"We stay out of sight and just see what we can see, yes?" Sally asked and he nodded. "Then I'm in."

"Me too," Mia said. "Christian needs medicine. The sooner we get this done, the sooner we can help him."

"Okay then," Glen said, "see that greenhouse there to the left? Mia, you start there and go left until you reach the main road. Do not cross that road unless you are absolutely certain no one can see you. Understand?"

Mia nodded and bit her lip.

"If you can cross it, go as far as the red barn. Sally, you start at the greenhouse and go right as far as the main road and then stop. I will cross the road way back into the woods and do the section on the other side. When you've seen all you can see, come back here."

They left their bags and rifle near the bivy and checked to see that Christian still was sleeping. Then Glen led the women back down the trail they'd arrived on, splitting off onto a smaller trail that led down the hill into the woods behind the town.

They stepped as lightly as they could and didn't speak. Glen felt hyper-alert and often stopped to listen. When they caught a glimpse of the greenhouse through the trees, he sent Mia left and Sally right. He moved back into the trees, taking a path through the undergrowth that should take him to the road, but farther from the town.

He moved quickly on his own, having developed the

ability to move silently through the woods while hunting. It was that, or starve to death. When he came to the road he spent a solid three minutes just listening. It seemed like forever, but he knew better than to rush. When the three minutes passed without the hint of a human sound, he crept to the edge of the road and listened again. He examined the road in both directions and then the woods around the road.

When he was completely certain he was alone, he crossed.

Back in the woods on the other side he switched direction and made for the edge of town, out where the red barn was. By now he hoped Sally had reached the road and was on her way back, Mia too, unless she'd crossed. Even then, she should be about ready to turn around.

He spotted the barn, but not Mia. He worked his way to the left, around the edge of the town, but still hidden by the woods. He spotted the fence he had noticed from above and, sure enough, there was a path that led to a gate into the yards behind the houses. You could build a fence, but you couldn't keep kids from exploring. And thank the powers that be for that.

Glen grinned and kept going. It was time to make his way back up to the ridge.

CHAPTER ELEVEN

SALLY AND MIA were waiting for him at the head of the game trail and they hiked back up to the ridge together. The women were quiet and Glen thought they looked exhausted. The whole group had to try getting better sleep. But not tonight, tonight was for burgling.

They stopped at the bivy to check in on Christian, who seemed feverish and restless. Glen told him to sleep a while longer and then led Sally and Mia away toward the top of the ridge again.

"Listen," he said. "There is a stream maybe a mile away. I'm going to see if I can collect some freshwater mussels. We all need some protein, and while you can live off travel bread for a really long time, it's best to have a little variety. You stay here and watch the town."

"What are we watching for?" Sally asked. She had circles under her eyes and she looked confused.

"Anything that might give us an advantage," he said. "The more information the better."

Glen looked back before they were out of view to see the girls hunkered down, heads close together as they kept watch on the town. He was relieved. That would keep them busy and, hopefully, they wouldn't start worrying about Christian. Glen was worried about Christian, and that was enough.

He quickly moved through a meadow of tall grass and then ducked back into the undergrowth. He was direction finding by memory, and listening hard for sounds of water. It took him thirty minutes, but he did find the creek where he remembered it. It was moving slow and easy, so it was no wonder he hadn't heard the water.

He took off his boots, stuffed his socks into them and then tied his laces together so he could hang them around his neck. He walked into the water, which reached mid-calf. He was being careful not to stir up the sand and silt he walked slowly along, scanning the bottom of the stream. It took a while, maybe ten minutes or so, for him to find the first mussel. He plucked it up, rinsed it in the slow moving water at the surface and dropped it in one of his boots.

He walked upstream for about twenty minutes, picking up mussels as he found them, then turned and made his way downstream, doing the same. On the way back up to the spot where he had entered the water he found another couple mussels he'd missed on the way down. So, when he climbed from the stream he had about forty mussels. Ten apiece. Not a feast, but with the travel bread enough to fill them up.

He dumped out his boots, dried his feet with his socks and put the socks and the boots back on. He had damp socks, but all in all it wasn't so bad. He took off his long-sleeved shirt, tied the mussels up in it and headed back to the others.

Thirty minutes later he was back at the ridge and emptying his shirt onto the grass. He waved to the women to stay where they were and began building a fire. He was careful to locate it where the townspeople wouldn't be able to see the smoke, a ways back from the edge of the cliff and down the hill. Any smoke would be hidden from the town by the hill and the woods. He would endeavor to make as little smoke as possible, but it was a fire after all. There would be smoke. He struck his hunting knife against the Ferro rod over a small pile of dry grass and twigs, and then fed the fire until he had a couple of small logs burning. Then he went in search of some greens – mostly Amaranth, clover and dandelion -and a couple of good pieces of bark.

When he returned the fire was burning hard. He prepared the mussels while it burned itself down to coals. He placed the greens on one of the pieces of bark, and then arranged the mussels on the greens. He covered the mussels with more greens, topped them with a second piece of bark and set them on the coals.

The bark immediately caught fire, which wasn't his goal, but wasn't horrible. With luck the greens would keep the flames from the mussels and they would steam and not get scorched. If they did get scorched, they would eat them anyway. He banked the coals around them and left them.

He made his way back to check on Christian, who he was worried about. As he feared, the infection was worse, red and oozing pus. Glen cleaned the wound the best he could, with Christian watching through wary eyes.

"It's not good, is it?" he asked.

"You just need antibiotics," Glen said. "But the town does not look welcoming. The plan is to sneak in tonight, take what we need, and sneak out again. But you don't need to come, the girls and I can make it without you."

"I'm coming," Christian said with his eyes closed. "There's no way I'm staying here while the three of you break into a town. No offense, Doc, but I'm the only one with any experience in breaking and entering."

"It's no good you coming if you are going to pass out. Your body is busy fighting this infection and you may find yourself passed out in the woods. That wouldn't be helpful."

"Feed me. Hydrate me. I'll be fine. I'm not staying here." Christian opened his eyes and gave Glen a look that told him not to bother arguing.

"Fine. It'll be on your head. Why don't you see if you can get up? We've got mussels for dinner." Glen left Christian to pull himself out of the tent and down to the fire.

Glen watched as Christian made his way down the hill. He was steadier than Glen expected him to be. Good. If he could be helpful, that would be a bonus.

Glen brushed the ash and greens off the mussels with a brush made of grass. The majority of the mussels had opened, so he picked up the ones that hadn't. He quickly tossed them in the coals, because they were hot and burned his fingers. If his bark platter hadn't burned, he would have been able to pull the others off the fire easily, but it had. So, he got smart and pulled out his hunting knife. He used the knife to flick the mussels into a pile of clover near the fire.

He whistled for the women, and they came down to join them. They all were quiet as they ate. Sally tore her bread open, pulled the mussels from their shells and made a mussel dandelion sandwich. Mia was a lot less bold, pulling the mussels from their shells and pretty much swallowing them whole, with a water chaser.

"You don't have to eat them if you don't like them," Glen said. "I won't be offended."

"I don't know if I like them or not," she replied, "but this way I get filled up without knowing."

"Why don't you try one and find out?" Glen asked, puzzled.

"Because, if I don't like them, I won't want to eat anymore, and we all need the protein. I'll try them when it won't matter if I like them or not." Mia shrugged her shoulders and went back to swallowing mussels whole.

"Fair enough," Glen said and went back to his own mussels.

Christian looked as if he was eating without an appetite. Chewing hard and swallowing without pleasure or hunger. He knew his body needed fuel, so he ate. Glen thought he could have put anything edible in front of Christian and he would have choked it down. You had to admire his determination, Glen thought.

When they all had finished, they gathered around what was left of the coals and talked town invasion as dusk fell.

"I think we should split into two teams," Glen said. "One team breaks into the pharmacy, while the other creates a diversion."

"Okay," Mia said. "How do we keep from getting caught if we're being diverting?"

"By making a bunch of noise, but not being seen," Glen said. "I bet Christian has some ideas about that."

"I do," Christian said. "We don't have any explosives, but we could light that tanker on fire."

"I think we should burn something closer to the village. They may not bother running down the road for a tanker that's a mile from the village, but light up a vehicle near one of the houses and they will come," Sally said.

"I take your point," Christian said. "We light an old pickup – something without a locked gas cap – the town runs to put it out, Mia and Glen sneak into the pharmacy, get what we need, and sneak out again. Right?"

"Yeah," Glen said, "but don't burn down any buildings, Okay? We don't want these people hunting us down."

"Are you sure we shouldn't just go up to the gate and tell them what we need?" Sally asked. "This way is so intrusive, and it's bound to piss them off."

"I just don't think we can risk it," Glen said. "We do that and they'll not only know who we are, but what we need. If they don't help us, we'll be out of luck. And we don't have time for negotiation. Christian needs antibiotics now. God knows what germs were in that river."

"I'm with Glen," Christian said. "I've got a limited shelf life. If we don't wrap this up tonight, I'm not going to be able to help."

"How bad is it?" Mia asked. "Can I see?" She reached over to lift his shirt, but he batted her hand away.

"Leave it," he said, and glowered at her.

But she wasn't looking at him, she was looking at his shirt. "Are you bleeding?" She looked closer at the stain that was growing on his shirt. "No. That's not blood." She leaned over and sniffed. "That's pus," she said. "You've already got an infection, don't you?" She turned angrily to Glen. "He's got an infection."

"Yes. He has an infection. Which is all the more reason for us to skip the pleasantries and cut to the chase. Christian wasn't kidding when he said he has one shot at this. If we don't get this treated by tomorrow, he'll be delusional from fever. I can continue cleaning the wound with boiled water, but I don't have what he really needs." Glen spread his hands in a gesture of need. "In fact, if they have any antiseptic, I wouldn't mind spraying that in there too. And super glue would be better than stitches at this point, as would butterfly bandages."

"That list is getting pretty dang long," Sally said. "Are we going to be able to create a big enough diversion?"

"Once in the pharmacy it shouldn't take more than five minutes to find what we need," Glen said. "The chaos created by a fire should more than cover that." He picked up a stick and drew a circle in the ashes on the outer edge of the dwindling fire.

"Here is the town," he said and drew a line through the middle of it. "And this is the main road running through it.

The pharmacy is here." He drew an X at the spot where Sally had noticed the pharmacy. Then he drew another X at the entrance to the town farthest from the first X. "This is the best area for starting a fire. It's the farthest point from the drugs."

He drew a dotted line in the ash from the edge of the woods to the place they were to start a fire. "Sally and Christian, you take my Ferro rod and my knife."

"I have my own knife," Christian said. "But I will need the Ferro rod."

"Great," Glen said. "Then Mia and I will go over the wall, here." He drew another dotted line to the place where they would breach the wall. "If it's quiet when we get there, then we'll go over before you start the fire. If there are people around, we'll wait."

"Hang on," Mia said, "Shouldn't I go with Christian? He needs me."

"You are smaller than Sally," Glen said. "You will be easier for me to boost over the wall. You are also a smaller shadow in the dark. It will be easier to keep you hidden. Sally can help Christian this time around."

"I don't like it," Mia said. "I don't like to be separated from him. It makes me nervous."

"It will be okay." Christian put a hand on her shoulder. "I promise I won't leave you behind. And anyway, Sally wouldn't let me."

She brushed his hand aside. "I'm not worried about you leaving me," she said. "I'm worried about you making it out of this alive. What if you collapse? Sally isn't strong enough to carry you."

Glen secretly thought that she wasn't strong enough either, as tough as she was. "Just for tonight, Mia," he said. "Sally and Christian are together, and you are with me. Okay?"

Mia looked at Christian. He and Sally both nodded at her, but she only appeared to notice Christian. "Okay," Mia said reluctantly, "you and I go over the wall. Then what?"

"Provided nothing goes wrong? We grab the stuff and run. Sally and Christian do the same. You only stay long enough to see that the fire is burning and then you run. We meet up on the trail and head straight back for the falls. They may or may not wait until morning to follow us, and we need to be long gone."

"So, we start our fire and leg it out of there. Come up the trail, I'm assuming Sally knows where the fork is that heads toward the falls?" Christian said.

Sally nodded and looked unhappy.

"We wait there for you and Mia and then we leg it. When do we head down?" Christian asked.

"Midnight," Glen said. "It will be fully dark, with a quarter moon to give us some light, but not too much light. We are fortunate not to have a full moon."

"Really?" Sally asked. "A full moon would be a bad thing?"

"On a night like tonight with no cloud cover? You bet." Glen said. "A full moon can seem almost like daylight under the right conditions. It's useless for cover."

"Huh," Sally said. "I guess I never went out at night and paid much attention."

"It wouldn't matter in a city," Glen said. "The ambient light – you know street lights and fluorescent signs – make the stages of the moon irrelevant. The night sky is a totally different animal in the city." He looked up at the swarm of stars above their heads. The moon only had begun topping the horizon and the stars were brilliant. He looked around and saw the others examining the sky as well.

"How could we have missed this?" Mia asked. "I don't think I've looked at the sky since we left the city."

"We've been too busy holing up at night," Christian said. "And if we were out, we were on the lookout for danger."

Sally dropped back in the grass, watching the sky above her. "Well I have two hours to make up for it now, but you probably should rest, Christian."

"Yeah, I'll sleep," he said. "But I'm not going back in that tent. I'll sleep out here under the stars with you."

CHAPTER TWELVE

IT WAS a little longer than two hours later when Glen shook Christian awake. He was hot to the touch and Glen worried that he might show symptoms of fever sickness, but he sat up, clear-headed and ready to go.

They collected all their belongings, Glen handing Christian the Ferro rod, and they started down the game trail. When they got to the point where the trail split, they stashed their bags in the grass on the side of the track and headed down the hill. It was dark under the forest canopy, where the moonlight couldn't reach, and so the going was slow. They didn't speak, and walked as quietly as they could, knowing that voices and footfalls carry.

At the base of the incline they split up, Glen and Sally going right to circle around to get to the road, and Glen and Mia going straight on. Glen chose what looked like a deer trail and led the way, placing Mia's hand on his shoulder so she could follow more easily.

When they were approaching the edge of the forest they stopped. They were to wait and watch, giving Christian and Sally time to make their way around the town, while also checking to see if people were out and about. Glen hunkered down with his back against a tree. The moonlight was illuminating the town just as he had predicted, and so far, there was no movement.

He looked over to see Mia lying on the ground, looking up through the branches. The canopy was less dense here and, glancing up, Glen could see a sea of stars. He smiled to himself. How like Mia to discover the night sky, and then spend every available moment examining it. He had best keep his eye on the town. What happened next would depend on what he could see.

A flicker caught his eye, and for a moment he thought he was seeing their diversion, but then he realized Main Street was illuminated by torches. It reminded him of illustrated scenes of eighteenth century London, with lanterns lining the streets. There was a certain romance to that century, which had been lost to the modern world. Well it was back, and Glen could do without the romance if it meant they had electricity again.

After about thirty minutes he tapped Mia on the leg to get her attention. It was time to go. She shook her head no and tapped her watch. He figured she wanted to wait longer, give the others time to set the fire. He pursed his lips and shook his head no. He jerked his head in a 'Let's go!' so sharp he about gave himself a headache.

Mia put her hands on her hips, which made him grin because she still was lying on her back and she looked ridiculous. He reined in the impulse to laugh and shook his head no. Then he pointed toward town with both his index fingers. She made an open gesture with her hands that clearly meant 'Oh my God, you are so stubborn. Can't you wait a few more minutes?' Glen crooked all four fingers on both hands, making sure she got his meaning of 'Get the hell up already. It's time to move.'

This time Mia shrugged and got to her feet. Apparently, the few minutes they'd spent playing charades had given the others the leeway she thought they needed. There was no fire, no call of alarm, but Mia got up anyway and followed Glen.

They encountered with a bramble bush as they came to the open area on the edge of the forest. Glen made a couple of tentative starts into the bush, but there wasn't a way through. So, they skirted the brambles and made their way under cover of the shadows to the concrete block wall that surrounded this end of the town. No lowly fence here, unfortunately, they would be scaling an eight-foot wall.

Why did they need a wall on this side of town? Was it the proximity of the cliff? Had they been attacked from above in the past? He led Mia along the wall, staying low so they didn't draw attention to themselves. Not that he'd seen movement in any of the upper windows. If he had, they wouldn't be here now.

It was hard to tell exactly where they were when they were so close to the wall, so Glen approximated the distance and stopped Mia at what he hoped was the right spot. After what seemed like several minutes, but probably was only seconds of frantic hand signals, she put her foot into his clasped hands and he boosted her over the wall. There was a dull thump and a whispered curse and then silence.

He tossed a length of rope over the wall and a moment later there was a tug. She was strong, he had to give her that. He was able to walk himself up the wall using the rope, and then swing himself over. They left the rope hanging on the wall in case a few seconds would make the difference on the way back.

Glen assumed they were in someone's backyard and was surprised to see a wind turbine. A small one, to be sure, but still it probably generated enough electricity on a windy day to power the house. He wondered if there were solar panels somewhere that he had missed. They weren't on the roof, he knew that. A glance along the row of backyards revealed many wind turbines. They may even have refrigeration here. Not that he didn't do okay with his pond and cold house. But still, electricity... that was civilization in and of itself.

They ducked down a passageway between the houses, being careful to listen for any sounds that would indicate someone knew they were there. The last thing he needed was to duck between two buildings and have a door open that would trap them there. They came out into a neighborhood of houses, crossed the street quickly, and ducked between two houses on the other side. They had five more rows of houses to get through before they reached the center of town.

A dog barked when they came out from between the next set of houses. They were in another set of backyards that backed onto the backyards of the houses on the next street. The dog was two or three yards down and seemed to have heard them. Glen reached out and pulled Mia up next to the wall, back in the space between the houses. It was dark, and if the dog didn't smell, then maybe he'd stop barking.

A door opened down the block and a woman's voice said, "Rocky, get in the house." And when the dog hesitated. "Now! Rocky!"

The dog went inside grumbling, and Glen and Mia stayed stock-still and silent for a few minutes more. But no other doors opened and no candles flickered in the windows. So, they started again, vaulting over the low wooden fence between the yards.

They reached Main Street without further mishap, and they were close to their objective. They'd overshot it by a few buildings, but it would take only a couple of minutes to reach the pharmacy. They jogged quietly down the street, staying to the shadows, and stopped in the dark doorway of the shop beside their objective. Glen listened. Nothing. There didn't appear to be any sort of sentries walking the streets. No one guarding the pharmacy. Nothing to keep them from breaking the lock and waltzing right in.

Which made Glen deeply suspicious. Here was a town using torches to light the streets, wind to power their homes. They'd seen fruit tree seedlings lining the streets and vegetable gardens in every yard. This was a place worth taking, so why was no one guarding it?

Mia was getting restless, but Glen made her wait. There was nothing to be gained by rushing into this. It was like their roles had reversed now that they were so close. She wanted to dive in, and he wanted to wait. It was ludicrous.

Light from the moon glinted off something on a roof across the street and startled Glen. What was that? And then it came to him. It was a solar water heater. Amazing. And now that he was looking, he spotted rigged solar panels as well. They weren't like any solar panel Glen had ever seen before. They were matt black, or at least they seemed so by the light of the moon. A new technology? Why not? Certainly any new tech that could be pirated or stolen would be.

He was impressed. Whoever was running this town was smart and capable. They knew what was needed to reinvent civilization. How many other towns across the country were doing the same? Thousands probably. And maybe he should go back to the little town near home and suggest it to them as well? How much better off they'd be with heat and refrigeration. He wondered if he could "borrow" a solar panel to examine.

Unlikely, but still, there had to be things they could do to transform their town like this one had done. Even if it was just basics – heat and light. Warm water and cold storage. He felt himself getting excited about the possibilities. They could get civilization back. Hot showers. Cold beer. Ice cream! It would take some effort and creativity, and imagination, certainly. But it was doable.

It didn't occur to him that he'd deliberately left civilization behind. That he hadn't wanted company or light or heat. Now that he saw it was possible, it was like the whole world had opened up to him again. Maybe it was time to stop playing Grizzly Adams and get back to the real world. He began hoping they did meet some people. This could be the beginning of a whole new life for him.

He could see Mia's face in the reflected moonlight and she was frowning. He bent and whispered so quietly it was hardly more than a breath, "What's wrong?"

"No diversion," she mouthed.

He shrugged. "Maybe they are having trouble lighting the Ferro rod," he mouthed back.

She looked at him in confusion and then shrugged, 'Whatever.'

They probably should move now, but he was strangely reluctant. He knew once they were in the pharmacy they'd have to move fast. There'd be no more examining the ways in which this town was coping. No, not just coping, thriving.

He took a last look around, taking in the details, and noticed that instead of grass in the stretch of earth between the sidewalk and the road, there was lettuce and other vegetables growing. Every inch of ground was being used. He began to feel guilty about all the yards they'd run through. Had they been running through the runner beans?

Was some poor family going to come out tomorrow morning to find their carrots and radishes trampled? He was looking around to see what else he might have missed in the dash to get here when Mia raised up on her tiptoes and whispered in his ear. "I think we'd better do this," she said. "I'm worried about Sally and Christian."

Of course, she had wanted to be teamed with Christian

and she was worried about him. Glen wasn't exactly worried, but he did wonder what had happened to their diversion. Luckily, the street was empty, and the entire town seemed to be asleep. So, why didn't they do this?

He nodded and took her hand. They ran quietly across the space between the buildings, crossing where the sliver of light from the moon was the narrowest. They were at the door to the pharmacy and, of course, it was locked. They'd expected that. Mia slipped a tool from her pocket and went to work on the door.

It didn't take but a moment for her to open the lock. This small town pharmacy hadn't bothered with high tech locks. There was the faint tinkle of the doorbell as she pushed the door open. They stepped through the doorway and let the door close behind them. They stood for a moment, letting their eyes adjust. Then a spotlight blinded them, and they were grabbed and held.

CHAPTER THIRTEEN

GLEN STRUGGLED, but Mia went limp. He wanted to urge her to fight, but one of the large men backhanded him and he could understand Mia's passive response to getting caught. "Wait!" Glen said, "I can explain."

"Oh, you'll explain alright," said the man holding the flashlight.

"We should take them to Terror," said the one holding Mia.

"We will, but I'd like to see what we have first. Mike, tie them up."

The guy behind Glen grunted and pulled his hands behind his back. Glen heard the buzz of a zip tie and his wrists stung as the nylon dug into his skin. Mike shoved him onto the floor in front of the checkout counter and went to snap a zip tie on Mia's wrists. A moment later she was on the floor with Glen, her face pinched in anger. She was going to spit nails or about to cry, and Glen couldn't tell which. He remembered how Sarah sometimes would cry when she was angry and how she hated that. "No one takes you seriously when you are crying," she would say. "I hate that."

He tried to smile at Mia, to let her know he thought they still could talk their way out of this, but she wasn't buying it. She glared at him. Did she blame him for getting them caught? He did. Why had it never occurred to him that someone could be waiting inside? And how had the men known he and Mia were coming? They couldn't have had a spy on the ridge with them. Could they? Had they been spotted checking out the town?

Glen wondered what he had missed. And how on Earth he had missed it. He was a surgeon, for God's sake. His whole job had been about details. And yet, here he was tied up and on the floor. At the mercy of three men who didn't look as though they had much pity.

Now that the spotlight wasn't in his eyes he could see them. They were big men, muscular and tattooed. Stereotypical Latino gang members, but Glen knew they all could hold degrees in nuclear physics. You just never knew. Just because they were big didn't mean they were dumb.

"Can I explain?" Glen asked. "We have..."

"Save it." This was Mike, the shortest man, with a tattoo of a dragon snaking down his arm to shoot flames across his hand. "Terror will deal with you."

Mia was silent, chewing on her lip and darting her eyes around the room. There were a lot of mostly empty shelves in the store and Glen could tell she was taking inventory of the contents. But what they needed wouldn't be in here. It would be in the back room, where the pharmacists spent the bulk of their time.

The three men had stepped away to have a quiet conversation and Mia struggled to her feet. She moved slowly down the counter and then down an aisle of cosmetics. Glen could see a tube of mascara still hanging from a hook. Mia was headed toward the back of the store, to where the medications were dispensed, when the big guy who appeared to be the leader of the three noticed that Mia wasn't where he had left her. He grunted to the guy with a third eye tattooed on his forehead to go find her.

As Third Eye walked past, Glen stuck out a leg and tripped the man. He went down hard and smacked his chin on the concrete floor. He bellowed and turned on Glen, but a word from their leader had him leaving Glen untouched and heading to the back of the store.

Glen hoped Mia had found what she was looking for. He had done what he could to help. He heard her yelp and started to his feet, ready to come to her rescue, but then Third Eye yelped louder and Glen relaxed. Mia was holding her own for the time being.

Third Eye appeared, pushing Mia along in front of him. He had a bruise forming on his left temple. "Head butt?" Glen asked.

Mia shook her head. "He grabbed my ass, so I kicked him," she said.

"I did not grab your ass!" Third Eye said, affronted. "It was an accident."

"Didn't feel like an accident to me," Mia said. She nodded to his bruise, "And maybe that will make you think twice next time."

"I did not grab her ass," Third Eye complained to the man Glen had dubbed 'Boss Man' in his head.

"See that you don't," Boss Man said. "If Maryellen finds out you've had your hands on another woman... well, let's just say I wouldn't like your odds."

"I did not," Third Eye said again. "I was going for her belt and she moved. Why would I grab this one's scrawny little ass when I've got Maryellen?"

"I'm sure that's what she'd want to know," Mike said. "But she won't hear it from me. I'm not interested in having my face slapped."

"Lock these two in the back," Boss Man said. "I don't want to have to worry about them while we figure this out."

"Get up," Mike said, flexing the hand with the dragon flames and making them dance. "I don't want to have to use this, but I will. And not to grab a piece of ass."

"I did not," Third Eye began.

"Shut it," Boss Man said. "Get those two in the back."

When they got to the back they realized the office had the kind of bolt lock with a key on the outside and a knob on the inside. They didn't have the key, and even if they did, Glen and Mia simply would turn the knob and be out. The bathrooms were the same. There were a couple of closets with no locks at all.

"We'll put them in the meds room," Mike said. "That door can be opened only from the outside."

And so Glen and Mia found themselves in the one place they actually needed to be. It took no time at all for Mia to find two different kinds of antibiotics. Glen was happy with the choice. If one didn't achieve the desired results, the other would. Mia slid packets of each into the waistband of her pants and pulled her T-shirt over them. Glen did the same. It was tricky with their hands tied behind their backs, but doable. Mia had a lot of flexibility.

She slid along the counter, her back to it, and started pulling open the drawers. She'd check the contents over her shoulder, and then move to the next. Glen wondered if she'd ever done this before, checked drawers with her hands tied behind her back.

"Yes!" she cried triumphantly, and pulled a box cutter from a drawer.

She examined it in her fingers for a moment, her eyes closed in concentration, then she clicked it open. She swiveled the knife in her hands and started sawing against the nylon cuffs, popping them off expertly without cutting herself. She caught Glen watching her.

"What?" she said. "Christian used to make us practice getting out of restraints. I've spent a lot of hours tied up." She pulled one packet of antibiotics from her waistband and slid it into the top of her socks. "Just in case."

She went to work on Glen's restraints and had them off in a moment. He rubbed his wrists while examining the medications on the shelves. He ignored the cooler. As much as he would have liked to have tetanus vaccine on hand, it had to be refrigerated and that made it pretty much useless to him.

He took additional antibiotics, painkillers, Benzodiazepines, and antiseptic. He also found gauze and sterile dressings. He took a plastic pharmacy bag, the kind the checkout person would put your purchases in, and he loaded it up, taped it closed and pushed it out through the bars in the window. With a little luck they could retrieve it later.

Mia still was rifling through the drawers, also shoving stuff into a bag, but he couldn't see what it was she was taking. Hopefully, it was something useful. He stood by the door listening while she continued rummaging around.

"I think I hear them," Glen said. He was pretty sure he'd heard the bell over the main door tinkle.

Mia quickly shoved her bag through the window and joined Glen at the door.

"Do we jump them as they come through the door?" she whispered. "Do we fight?"

He thought a moment. "No. I don't think we can take all of them. Pretend you still have your cuffs on. We'll wait for a moment when we can run."

She ran to pick her broken cuffs up off the floor, the box knife and some medical tape. "Here, tape me back together."

He took the broken cuffs and taped them back together,

hiding the spliced parts between her back and wrists. "Don't yank too hard on them," he said. "They won't hold."

The key turned in the door and he dropped the knife and tape on the counter and held his own hands behind his back. He didn't have much hope they wouldn't notice he wasn't cuffed, but it seemed like the thing to do. Then he changed his mind and dropped his hands.

"What are you doing?" Mia hissed in her no-good-will-come-of-this tone.

"Just an idea," he said as the door opened. "Wait and see." And he dropped his hands to his sides, palms outward.

The door slammed open, and Mike and Third Eye stood filling the doorway. "What's this?" Mike said, looking at Glen.

Glen lifted his arms slightly from his side, a sign of submission. "Sorry," he said. "My cuffs came off." The men swarmed him and had him re-cuffed in seconds flat.

"Could you please let me tell you why we're here?" he asked. He noticed that they'd cuffed him tighter this time. His gambit hadn't paid off.

Third Eye gave Mia's cuffs a quick look, but didn't notice they'd been taped on. "Why didn't you take her cuffs off?" he said. "Don't trust her?" He gave Mia a little shove out into the main store.

"Didn't have time," Glen said. "I was too busy looking for uppers."

"Uppers? No one's used that term since the seventies." Mike laughed. "You wouldn't find crack in here."

"No dude," Third Eye said, "people still say uppers, although E or crack might be more popular. You still can get uppers."

"Whatever, man," Mike said, glaring. "It doesn't matter now, does it? You aren't going to find E, crack, or uppers anywhere around here. New York, maybe. Not in Terror Town."

"No, man, I bet you could find some Adderall in here if you looked hard enough. I had a cousin who was hooked on Adderall in high school. Had to have it." Third Eye started nodding his head for emphasis.

"So, this other kid faked ADH, ADO, he faked not being able to concentrate, and then sold my cousin his pills. I thought it was a good deal. But never could get the doc to prescribe them for me. Kind of a letdown." He looked at his fingernails. "But I bet they've got some in here."

"We don't need uppers," Glen said. "I was kidding. We just need..."

"Save it," Boss Man said from the doorway. "Bring them out here."

Mike and Third Eye pushed them over to the bench where people used to sit and wait for their prescriptions. It was covered with smeared dust, but so was Glen, so that didn't bother him. He just observed the dirt and sat down, leaning slightly forward so his hands didn't get trapped between his body and the wall.

Mia was doing a good job looking miserable, and even let a few tears drip down her face. Not that she didn't have reason to cry, but he'd gotten to know her well enough that he doubted that's what was going on. She was keeping the thugs off-balance, or if not off-balance, feeling as though she wasn't that much of a threat. He wondered if Third Eye would forget he got kicked in the face. Not likely, but he might think it was a fluke.

"Before I take you to Terror, I have a few questions," Boss Man said. "How did you find us?"

"We walked two days south, looking for a town with a pharmacy. Luckily, we came across that ridge out there." He nodded toward the cliff. "We looked over and there you were."

"Is that right?" Boss Man asked Mia.

Glen wished he'd taken the time to go over their story with Mia. They would need consistency to be believed.

"Sounds right to me," Mia said. "We walked for two days. When we woke up the sun was on our left and at night it disappeared on the right. So, unless we're in Australia, we walked south."

"How many more of you are there?" and when Glen started to answer he held up a hand. "I want her to answer."

"There are four of us altogether," Mia said.

Boss Man looked at Glen and Glen nodded yes.

"And the other two?" Boss Man asked Mia.

"Christian got savaged by a bear," Mia said. "They are back at camp – Sally's looking after him."

Again Boss Man looked at Glen, and again he nodded in the affirmative.

"And you," Boss Man looked at Glen again, "what did you do for a living before the end?"

"Neurosurgeon," Glen said succinctly.

"Student," Mia said.

"And you were able to help your friend, what's his name, Christian?"

Mia nodded.

"So, you could help Christian because you are a surgeon?"

It was Glen's turn to nod. He was hopeful they'd be able to work this out, or if not, get themselves free and pick up what they'd taken on the way out. These men didn't seem unreasonable, just big and protective. Just what you'd expect of people trying to keep their community safe. They weren't necessarily radical or terrorists, although they kept talking about taking them to Terror, whatever that meant. So, maybe he was wrong, and they were terrorists.

Glen's spirits sank. What if he was wrong about these people and there would be no dialog? What would happen to them? Were intruders killed in this community? Were they integrated, sent away? What?

"What are you going to do with us?" The words slipped out almost of their own accord. "Because there is a man dying up the hill. And if we don't live, he certainly won't. So tell me, man, what are you going to do?"

"I don't know," Boss Man said. "I'm not in charge here. My job is to get information about what you are doing here and then take you to the guy who is in charge. That's all. What are your names?"

Glen bit back a smart reply. He wasn't the one with the power in this situation, and the quicker they got through this bullshit and got to the person who actually could help, the better. "Glen and Mia," he said with a sigh. Such a waste of time.

"Glen and Mia who?" Boss Man asked.

"Glen Carter and Mia..." Glen thought a moment. "I'm sorry, Mia, I don't remember your last name."

"Mia Clemo," she said. "I don't think I ever told you."

"So, you haven't been together long?" Boss Man asked.

"Just because you don't know someone's last name doesn't mean you haven't been together for a while," Glen said, even though in this case it did mean that. "Last names just aren't important anymore."

"That true, that," one of the other two men said behind Glen's back. "Last names don't mean shit anymore. I don't even remember mine."

Glen doubted that was true, but the conversation got Boss Man off-track and maybe he wouldn't ask how long he and Mia really had been together. It seemed important that the illusion of solidarity and history be maintained. He felt they were particularly vulnerable to being turned on each other.

"So, Glen and Mia are here getting medicines for Christian, who was savaged by a bear and is being watched over by Sally. Is that correct?" Boss Man asked.

"Pretty much," Glen said as Mia nodded. Except maybe the bear part, that could have been Mia or Sally, but he wasn't going to tell these people that.

"And you have no other motive other than to get antibiotics?" Boss Man asked.

"No," Glen and Mia spoke at the same time and looked at each other, startled.

"Well, that was fun," Boss Man said. He nodded to Third Eye and Mike, "get them up and bring them."

"We going to Terror now?" Third Eye asked.

"We're going to Terror," Boss Man agreed.

CHAPTER FOURTEEN

THE THREE MEN led Glen and Mia out of the pharmacy and down the street. People started appearing on porches, watching them pass by. Families were joined by their neighbors from other streets, standing on the sidewalks or perched on the porches.

The stares weren't all hostile, Glen noticed. Some were simply curious. Others, especially children, were afraid. A couple of people looked excited, which could have been a good thing, as in 'Look, new people to befriend,' or a bad thing, as in 'Look, new people to terrify and then murder.' It was impossible to tell which it was.

A bored-looking teenager was tossing what looked like a tomato up in the air and catching it in a very measured way. Glen felt sure he was going to lob it at Mia, but before he could tell her to get behind him, Mike caught his eye and shook his head. The boy looked disappointed, but dropped the tomato.

After that, the walk through town was fairly uneventful. Somehow news traveled that they weren't to be assaulted, although no one spoke, so Glen didn't know how that news was communicated. He saw barking dogs pulled back into their houses or backyards, and a number of people went with them.

The air had a snap in it that he hadn't noticed earlier when his adrenaline had been running high. Now he shivered and he noticed goose bumps on Mia's arms as they passed beneath a torch. Fall really was setting in, and the people on their lawns and porches were wearing sweaters and jackets. Some had zippered sweatshirts with the hoods pulled up.

He heard something odd and glanced back to see the town falling into line behind Boss Man, Third Eye and Mike. The entire freaking town was escorting them to wherever it was they were going. Crowds of people were strange, Glen reflected. They didn't act like normal human beings.

He thought of the last time he'd walked through his neighborhood in Philly, before everything had gone so wrong in his life. People had waved and smiled. Some asking after his family. That's what people were like. Friendly and open. Crowds, he shuddered at the thought of the hoard behind them, they were unpredictable. The group mentality. He hoped this crowd was as easily controlled as they seemed to be.

They walked almost the entire length of the town before they turned and passed an elementary school. There were swings, slides, and hopscotch markings on the blacktop. He wondered if the children still attended school in this town. Were there any teachers here?

Past the school there was a large stone and concrete block building with a number of torches lighting the front. "Library" had been inscribed over the door and it seemed as though this was where they were heading. Boss Man directed them up the stairs to the front door and followed them with Mike and Third Eye. The rest of the town gathered in the street, not crossing the sidewalk onto the garden. Here, like most places, the lawn was broken up by raised beds.

Mike pulled the huge door open and ushered them inside. They were standing in a huge foyer, several stories high. The floors were marble and sparkled like they'd been polished yesterday. For all Glen knew they had been polished recently. Maybe that's how people kept busy, by keeping the public buildings spic and span. Boss Man gestured to an open doorway to the right and he, Glen and Mia went in, while Mike and Third Eye stood sentry outside the door.

This space looked to Glen like a huge reading room. There were shelves, just like in any library, but the center of the room was devoted to tables and chairs, with the occasional armchair slid into nooks. There was a seating area around a fireplace at the far end of the room, and that's where the sole occupant was seated. The fire in the fireplace was burning and silhouetted against the flames was the figure of a man in an armchair, reading.

The man in the armchair was Tyrell Moore, a tough ex-military man who had earned the moniker 'Terror" for his ferocity while serving in Iraq and Afghanistan. He survived ten years in the army before coming home to train soldiers to deal with civil unrest. He prided himself on being tough in body and mind. He didn't take shit from anyone.

He watched from his chair as Javier, his second in command, directed his captives to approach, but before they could get three-quarters of the way across the room he rose from his chair and went to meet them. He preferred to meet intruders on his terms, away from the comfortable couches and welcoming fire.

He took stock of the pair as they approached each other. A tall man. Not military in bearing, but disciplined and well-muscled in the way tall thin men could be. Beginning to gray at the temples. He looked hopeful.

The girl was young, early twenties he thought, blonde, blue-eyed, and not tall like the man, but short and tight, like a fighter. She looked angry. Terror found that very interesting.

They were both filthy. Like they been soaked in the rain and rolled in the dirt. His hair was short, so the fact it was unkempt didn't matter so much, but her hair was matted and full of twigs and leaves. They'd come through the forest, not down the road. Terror didn't think they were related, and probably didn't know each other that well. There was some distrust there.

She watched him warily, but he barely glanced in her direction. All the man's attention was focused on Terror, and there was hope in those eyes. He was hoping to encounter a sympathetic man. Terror would have to put the hope to rest, the sooner the better. Terror was not a man to rule with empathy.

They wanted something, and Terror either would be able to give it to them, or not. At the moment he thought not. The question was what to do with them after they'd been disappointed by his answer. Keep them or throw them away? Kill them or let them go? Those were the choices. Would either of them be any use to him? The man possibly, depending on his skills. The woman? As a breeder perhaps. She was very fit, so perhaps she could work in security or construction. He'd have to see. She'd need to lose the anger if she was to be any use at all.

Something about her reminded him of his own mother. She'd been a dark-haired woman, once beautiful, at least he'd remembered her that way. But the stress and worry of the living in the projects had aged her. She had not married his father, never married at all. She was fiercely independent, but raising children alone is not easy. There were times when he came home from school to find a new man in the house. It never lasted long. Either Tyrell did something the man didn't like, or his mother did. They'd stomp out angrily, as if they would have stayed if only Tyrell and his mom hadn't ruined it. Even then Terror knew bullshit when he saw it.

And then she had fallen in with some guy who had promised to help her out, but he'd only rented her body to men from the street. His mother had gone downhill, using drugs and alcohol to dull the humiliation and pain of finding herself a prostitute. Young Tyrell had run and he'd ended up in the place least like the projects that he could find. The military.

He remembered his mother's face the day he left. She was angry, like this woman. Betrayed by a man once again. A bruise on her cheek and a cast on her arm, broken by the man who'd professed to love her. Tyrell doubted she was still alive, but if he ran into that pimp again he would be dead before he knew what hit him. And that was God's truth.

Something about the way the man walked reminded Terror of the doctor who'd put him back together after an IED had gone off next to a transport he'd been riding in. They had the same bearing. The military doc had been tough. He'd laid it out for Terror, plain and simple. Either work through the pain and force his body back into its former condition or be discharged. Those were the choices.

Terror had chosen the hard route, and that damn doctor had been there every inch of the way, goading Terror on. Pushing him to the limit and the pushing him some more. He never gave up on Terror, and Terror never gave up on himself. He pushed himself through the pain and got his body back. He may have been even stronger than before. He was on active status for two more years after he was shipped back to his unit. Two years of all-out war. He'd given it his best and would have stayed longer, but everyone has to come home sooner or later.

He'd come back stateside and was planning to retire when

he heard the podcast that changed his life. It was about the effects of an Electrical Magnetic Pulse, otherwise known as an EMP, on America. He still could remember the sound of the commentator's voice.

"The collapse of the United States will be complete. If this EMP blast were detonated in the Midwest, most of the North American continent would feel its effects, and we would be thrust back into the seventeenth century. North Korea is counting on the demise of America, and you'd better be ready.

Only the blast hadn't come from North Korea, it had been a storm from outer space. And North Korea had been just as affected as the rest of the world, according to the ham radio operators.

Soldiers had gone AWOL from the army, many trying to make their way back to their families. But Terror didn't truck with that. He went hunting, dragging as many AWOL soldiers back to the army as he could find. What the army did with them was their concern.

And because of that podcast he'd been ready. The army pretty much had fallen apart without technology, but not Terror. He had planned and he was ready. This town was only one of many he'd created across the United States, and he had plans to make many more. He would continue converting backward, powerless towns into mini-civilizations, with power and food. Places where children could be raised in safety.

Because that was his plan, to build an America that was safe for women and children. A place were neither was bought or sold. Where every person had enough to eat, every adult had a job to do, and no child was getting beaten just for being there. He would bring safety and compassion, strength, and understanding.

But to do that he had to maintain the reputation of a badass who had no mercy. He pulled his mind back to the matter at hand. What to do with this pair of intruders? Who would they want to meet? The level-headed leader, of course, a man who could be reasoned with. So, what would he give them? The Terror.

He pulled a tomahawk from his utility belt, and as the two approached, he whipped it around and caught the man across the back of the neck, pulling him close until they were face to face. "They call me Terror," he said. "What are you doing in my town?"

CHAPTER FIFTEEN

THE COLD STEEL against the back of Glen's neck was painful, and he felt fear-filled adrenaline rush through every cell of his body. He hadn't felt fear since the accident. The cold metal on his neck had the same effect as the eighteen-wheeler screaming up the wrong side of the road. He felt sick to his stomach, but pulled a deep breath in through his nose. And another, until he felt calm enough to speak.

"We need antibiotics for a man who is injured," Glen said. He was careful to keep every word precise. Christian wasn't precisely a friend, so he wouldn't call him that. There was no room for lies in a situation like this.

"Where is this injured man?" Terror asked.

"Outside of town," Glen replied. "We didn't bring him with us. He's with another woman who is supposed to be keeping an eye on him. He was attacked, by a bear, I think, and I'm pretty sure he's going to go into septic shock and die if I don't get those antibiotics to him."

"And why is this so important to you? Is he related to you in some way?" Terror asked, his eyes cold and calculating.

"I'm a doctor," Glen said," a surgeon. Three people

showed up on my doorstep, the man was bleeding profusely from a gut wound. I couldn't turn them away. I might have been the only person who could help within one hundred miles. I couldn't in good conscience turn them away. Could I?"

Terror kept quiet, looking steadily into Glen's eyes.

Glen found it unnerving, but he looked steadily back. Proving he was telling the truth and willing this man to believe him. He wished Terror would release the tomahawk. It hurt, and he wished he could put his hand back there to see if he was bleeding. But he stood still and gazed into the dark brown eyes, waiting for the verdict.

"He's telling the truth," Mia said, having finally found her voice. "We came here for medicine. When we saw all the barricades, we thought it would take too long to try explaining, so we snuck in. We weren't going to take much, just enough antibiotics to save Christian."

This was a lie, and Glen wished she'd just left out that detail. Never lie if you don't have to do so. He didn't know how he knew this was true, but he did. Do not let them catch you in a lie. Because if they do, they won't believe anything else you say.

Terror's eyes flicked away to examine Mia and then back to Glen. "Is that true?" he asked.

"About ninety percent true," Glen said.

"Once we saw everything you had, I'm not sure we could have resisted taking some painkillers and sterile bandages as well. But the original plan was to take just the antibiotics." He hoped Mia didn't feel betrayed, but he didn't dare lie to this man. He still had hope Terror would let him go.

The eyes flicked to Mia again. "That true?" Terror asked.

"Yes," Mia replied, "that's true."

"You see anything else you wanted in there?" Terror asked.

"Yes, birth control pills," Mia said. "Rape and pregnancy are a real risk out there."

"That is true," Terror said, and his gaze flicked back to Glen. He slid the tomahawk from behind Glen's neck.

Glen straightened and rubbed the back of his neck. No blood. So, Terror knew exactly how much pressure to exert. He felt the beginnings of a sigh of relief and held it back. A sigh would be a display of weakness, and he didn't dare show that either.

Terror turned to Mia and started grilling her about her experience as a woman before and after the end. Glen, who had heard this all before, let his mind slip back. What was Sara's experience as a woman, he wondered. He'd assumed it was good, that she'd had everything she wanted and was sheltered from abuse. But was that true?

He thought about Sarah. When he first had met her she'd had ambitions. Things that she wanted to do with her life. It had seemed easy and natural for her to give them up when Clarence was born. But maybe that was just his perspective. Had she resented being left at home with a toddler while he went off into the world every day?

Did she secretly yearn to be free of him? Were her days spent online looking for the life she had planned for? Clarence wasn't a demanding child, maybe she didn't spend all her time playing with the boy, as he had assumed.

He found himself short of breath at the thought that Sarah might have resented him. He took a couple of breaths as surreptitiously as he could to calm himself. What was he doing working himself into a lather over the past when the present was so dangerous? He knew the human mind had a tendency to redirect when it found the present too stressful, but he should know better. If there was a time in his life he needed to be present, it was now.

Terror still was talking with Mia. In fact, it seemed not

many minutes had gone by, since she still was explaining her need for birth control.

"Not only that," she was saying, "women die giving birth, even with all the modern monitors and what not. Now that those things are unavailable more women will die in child-birth. I'm just not interested. Can you imagine the irony, to get pregnant because you've been raped, and then to die giving birth to that child? Yeah. Not for me."

"But what makes you think you will be raped?" he asked. "You can't protect yourself, maybe, but what about the men in your party?"

"Like the one who is currently dying because he was too stupid to run away from a bear?" she asked. "We can't rely on anyone anymore. If we go into a town as a group asking to trade for something, we don't have anything they want. They have plenty of men, so they don't need labor or security. Then that leaves women. Even if Christian was to say no, we very well could be overpowered."

"I supposed that could be true," Terror said. "I have seen a lot of brutality in my time."

"And then there's getting your period." She glanced up and saw the look of aversion on Terror's face. "Sorry, I forget guys don't like talking about women's physical issues. I'll just say that birth control pills can make it stop. Right, Doc?"

"They can indeed," Glen said.

"That eliminates the need for a whole lot of feminine products, to say nothing of leaving a blood trail for every predator to follow." She shrugged. "So, are you going to kill us, or what?"

Terror laughed.

Glen backed up a step in confusion. Was that a genuine laugh? It didn't sound like the laugh of an evil maniac getting ready to do someone in.

"Not today," Terror said. "But I still must think what to

do with you and your dying friend in the woods. Please have a seat while I discuss this with my men."

"Can we have our hands untied?" Mia asked. "It's really uncomfortable to sit like this."

Glen shot her a look. Had she forgotten her hands were just taped together? She caught his eye and bit her lip. She had forgotten.

"No." Terror had not noticed her confusion. "Do I look stupid?"

One of the men laughed and Terror shot him a look that shut him up. "Stay put," he said to Mia and Glen. "We'll be back in a minute." He motioned to his men to follow him into the hallway.

The second they were out of the room Glen leaned forward to whisper to Mia. "We both are not going to be able to escape. So, if the opportunity comes, you need to run for it. There's an exit sign down there at the end of the room. Your hands are already free. You run and I'll knock over anyone who comes after you, okay?"

"No way am I leaving you here." Mia's cheeks flushed as she spoke. "After everything you've done for us. It's just not happening."

"Listen, Christian can die if he doesn't get those capsules. You have to run when you get the chance, because we don't know when we'll get the opportunity again. You hear me? You are his only chance for survival." Glen glared at Mia. He didn't know how to make her understand how serious the situation was for Christian. "I'm serious, Mia. He needs medicine now."

"But what if they kill you? I'll have that on my conscience for the rest of my life. You think I could stand that? Knowing that I'd left you to die?" A tear ran down her face.

Glen wanted to remind her that just a week ago they'd been ready to kill him for the stuff in his cabin, but he didn't.

"There is no sense in both of us dying," he said. "If they start killing, it won't be just me. So we are saving you and Christian. Got it?"

Her lower lip quivered.

"I'm good at talking my way out of things. If it looks as though they're going to bump me off, I'll bargain with them. Having a surgeon in house will look pretty appealing to them. I guarantee you. So, at the very worst, you'll run away thinking I'm stuck in this town for the rest of my days. But that's not such a bad thing. They have food and medicine, and hey – refrigeration. I could have cold beer. So, go and don't feel sorry for me. My life will be easier than yours."

"I still don't know," Mia started.

"Hush," Glen said. "I don't want them to hear us talking."

The conversation in the hallway had died down and Glen expected them to return any moment. It was then that church bells started ringing furiously.

CHAPTER SIXTEEN

THERE WERE CONFUSED yells from the entryway. A door slammed open and someone yelled "Fire at the north entrance!"

Finally, Glen thought, our diversion.

"Go now!" Glen hissed at Mia, not wanting to alert the men sooner than needed. "Run!"

She took off like a shot. She may have been short, but she had a lot of speed in those legs.

Glen heard Terror yell, "Go back and watch the captives!" A second later, Third Eye ran back into the room. It took him no time at all to spot Mia tearing for the exit and he started after her. Glen launched himself from the chair, driving his shoulder into the man's midsection. They went down in a heap. Glen was on top of Third Eye and tried trapping him by wrapping his legs around Third Eye's midriff.

He was partially successful. He managed to delay Third Eye for a few precious seconds before the man shook him off and went running after Mia. Mia was long gone by that time, and Glen hoped she was able to stay out of his clutches. He sat back down in his chair and waited for the inevitable punishment.

It was a while coming. First, Third Eye came back and kicked out at Glen as he passed on his way out the front. The kick missed. Mike came in and sat in a chair near the door, keeping an eye on Glen. Glen could have told him not to bother. As long as he didn't try escaping, Mia was probably safe. If Glen tried to escape too, then they'd probably hunt them both down. So, he stayed put, closing his eyes and catnapping in the silence.

He did wonder what was happening in the outside world. For a while, through the open window he could hear yelling and people running, but after a while it all calmed down. Glen let his chin drop down to his chest and rested. He would have loved to lean back or lie down, but with his hands behind his back the discomfort made it not worth it.

He was dozing when Terror came back in and roughly shook him awake. "Hmm?" he mumbled. He couldn't rub his eyes with his hands, so he rubbed his face on his upper arms. He blinked at Terror, who was standing over him, clearly angry.

"Did you know about that little stunt?" Terror asked.

"I did." Glen nodded slowly. He was so very tired.

"And what did you think to accomplish by burning one of our vehicles?"

"It was just a diversion, only it came too late. Or maybe we came too early. We should have waited, but the pharmacy looked empty and the streets were quiet, so we went ahead." Glen felt the gloom overtake him. He'd planned correctly, but his follow through left a lot to be desired. At least Mia was free.

"Did the girl take medication back to your friend?" Terror asked.

"That was the plan," Glen said. "If she didn't make it, another man will die."

"One may die anyway," Terror said. "One of my men was severely burned putting out that fire."

"I'm sorry to hear that," Glen said. He couldn't bring himself to look Terror in the eye. "I hope he recovers."

"Too bad you aren't a burn doctor," Terror said. "Since you're not, and I'm tired of dealing with you, this is your punishment for not being upfront with me." He raised a pistol and struck Glen on the back of the head.

Glen saw a burst of light, felt searing pain, and then everything went black.

CHAPTER SEVENTEEN

Mia was running with everything she had. Luckily, almost everybody in the town already had run to the fire and weren't looking in their backyards to see her hopping over fences and dodging around raised garden beds. She knew it was crazy, but she didn't want to trample anyone's garden. Food sources were too important to trample on. And she was fast and could afford an extra step or two.

She ran behind the houses, one block over from the library. It had been tricky getting there, first tearing out of the library and running along the fence behind the elementary school, all the while afraid that any second now one of Terror's men would grab her by the neck. She'd heard one of them come out the same exit she had. So, she'd thrown herself on the ground and rolled under a hedge. When she heard him thunder off in the wrong direction she'd rolled back out from under the hedge to find a German shepherd staring her in the face.

She'd frozen, remembering the pain of a dog bite from her childhood, but the dog had sniffed her and wandered off to raise his leg on the chain-link fence. She nearly burst into tears with relief but reined it in and started running again. The dog ran with her for about a block, but when she stopped to see if she could safely cross over into the next block, he'd wandered off to sniff something else.

That was good. It was hard enough keeping her own footfalls quiet. She'd waited until a child down the block had disappeared inside a house before dashing across the pavement and between two homes. That was when she started vaulting fences.

She needed to get in line with the pharmacy, but she wasn't positive how far down it was. She briefly considered not picking up the supplies she and Glen had pushed through the window. But she had to go back for Christian. His wounds already were infected and he needed the antibiotics. Dollars to dimes there wouldn't be anyone watching it now.

She heard running footsteps coming her way and dropped into the dirt behind a compost pile. She was lying in rotting vegetables. The footsteps passed on the street and she got up, not bothering to wipe away the mess on her shirt and pants. Better to be stinky than dead.

Another couple of fences and she landed in a yard of chickens, lots of chickens. She stopped and picked her way slowly around the cackling hens. She was about halfway across the yard when a rooster flew up and grabbed at her hair with his talons. He latched onto her back, piercing her jacket. She swung around, batting at him until he dropped off. She ran, scattering chickens who squawked and either moved away or pecked at her feet. The rooster regained his equilibrium and came after her again. She booted him with the side of her foot, like a soccer ball. He flew across the yard, feathers flying, landed and stayed there for a minute before getting up and shaking his feathers.

Mia didn't feel bad about booting him. Her back was stinging where he had scratched her, and she'd have to get

Sally to clean it so it didn't get infected. Damn bird. She tried resuming her previous speed, but she was in pain now and every jolt made her wince. She must be getting close to the pharmacy by now.

She slid out from between two houses, checked both ways, and jogged across the street. She ran across both backyards, there was no fence she had to vault, for which she was grateful. She thought she might be on Main Street now, so she slipped between the houses more slowly, stepping as quietly as she could. She was right. She recognized the houses facing her, but she was temporarily disoriented and couldn't decide which way to go.

Had she overshot the pharmacy? But no. If she'd gone too far, she wouldn't have recognized the houses. She trotted up the sidewalk, keeping close to the buildings. Then she recognized the doorway where they had waited to approach the pharmacy. She ran up the alley between the pharmacy and the store. The bags still were there. She scooped them up, turned and almost ran right into a young man standing on the sidewalk watching her.

She stopped, heart beating fast and hard, mind panicking. Should she try disabling him, or pretend that she lived there? Surely everyone must know everyone else in this town?

"What are you doing," he asked, looking puzzled.

"Forgot something," Mia said, and dodged past him, across the street and over the town square.

She darted around what must be the town hall, she decided, and stopped listening for cries or running feet over the pounding of her heart. No sound of pursuit. She dropped all attempts at concealment and ran right down the middle of the street in the direction of the wall. She could see it in front of her, an immovable object, and a dead end running across the street and behind the houses.

It was too tall for her to climb. She looked for something

to use as a ladder. There was nothing. As she approached the wall, breathing hard, she swore under her breath. This could be the end of her. The rope was somewhere behind the houses, and even if she found it, there was nothing to attach it to.

She looked over the fence behind the house to the right. Nothing there to help her, same on the left. She was about to give up and start running behind the houses when she laughed out loud. She could climb the fence and then get over the wall. She quickly walked to the place where the wall and fence met and tossed her bags over. Then she climbed the chain-link fence, hefted herself onto the top of the wall and slid over it, hanging by her fingers until she dropped.

The ground was not forgiving. She landed on her feet, lost her balance, and sat down hard, catching herself with the palms of her hands. The pain brought tears to her eyes, but she got up and grabbed the bags, which were on the ground nearby. Her palms were bleeding. She wiped one, then the other – switching the bags from one hand to the other – to remove the dirt and rocks.

Then she started off again, sticking to the road for the time being. Her run had become a slow jog and she was limping. But out here it was dark and it would be hard to see her under the shadow of the trees. She would stick to the road for as long as she could.

Terror was sitting in the same place he had been when Glen and Mia first had been brought to him. He'd had his men drag Glen down to the courthouse to be housed in one of the cells. He'd hit Glen pretty hard, but he didn't doubt the man would recover by morning. He'd have a hell of a headache for a day or two, but so what? He should be happy he was still alive.

Terror was furious that the girl had escaped, but not foolish enough to send men out looking for her. Even when the sun came up, there were far too many places a person could hide in the forest, and if they all went out there, there was nothing to keep her from coming back here and releasing Glen. He had plans for Glen.

There was a general practitioner in town, but he was aging and never had been a surgeon. A child had died of appendicitis the year before because the doctor had no experience with removing one. He had tried and the child had not recovered. A real surgeon in trade for a few medical supplies, now that was a bargain.

The problem would be getting the doctor to cooperate. Men who were forced into service were never as reliable as those who joined voluntarily. He'd need a good reason to stay if he wasn't to spend every waking hour planning his escape.

Terror would have to find out what it was this doctor wanted from life and then offer it to him. Or something close enough that he'd be willing to give up his current life, whatever that was, to live in the community. And maybe community would be enough. But he'd have to find out. It was too much trouble constantly guarding members of the community. They'd tried doing that with the local police force when they first had taken over and it hadn't worked.

They'd tried threatening one officer's family, but the entire lot of them had planned an escape. In the end he'd let them go, but he told the town he'd executed them. He had to maintain his reputation as a hardass, but he'd never been one to kill innocents. And those children never would have survived out there without their father. It was hard enough to be raised by one parent in a civilized world. But this one? No way. He wasn't going to be responsible for that.

He knew it was a weakness, this inability to kill indiscriminately and for no purpose but his own good. He never had been one to punish those who had done nothing more than try staying alive in a cruel world. Those who targeted innocents, though, they were fair game. Those who showed cruelty, who used women against their will, who tortured animals, those were the men Terror hunted. He hunted them and he killed them. There was no mercy for those who discarded their humanity.

Eventually, he'd given everyone in this town a choice, stay and live in a safe but autocratic society, or leave. Most of the families had stayed. Many of the unattached men had left. Once gone, no one came back. Not that he'd offered them that choice, but if anyone had returned, he would have considered repatriating them. If they'd come back by choice, they'd be good for morale. And they would tell stories of the outside, which would serve to teach his community how lucky they were.

But the doctor, Terror had the feeling he was going to be a hard case. He wondered what the doc's story was. Maybe if he could get to know him, the doc would be willing to tell him. If Terror could find his vulnerabilities, then perhaps he could convince the doctor to stay. That would be far easier than keeping him in a cell or having to post a 24-hour watch on him.

He folded the map he'd been studying when the thieves had been brought to him. His eyes were tired, it must be getting close to dawn and he'd spent a lot of time calming his people down after the fire. Not the men he had brought with him, but the families that had stayed in the town when Terror had arrived. They were afraid for their children. In the end, Terror had explained to them about the doctor and his companions and pointed out how the fire had been set in such a way that none of the buildings had been at risk. It was just a diversion.

Still, he would have to consider what to do to strengthen the town's defenses. Institute a night patrol for the perimeter, for one. That had been very effective when raiders had come at his other towns. A night patrol and guard towers, one at each end of the town. That would give some of the younger men an occupation. Those boys, young men who might have been away at college if the world hadn't come to an end, were restless and tended to cause trouble because they had nothing better to do.

He'd start them building guard towers in the morning. He'd assign border patrol to some of the steadier men. And then he'd see what he could do with that doctor. He stood up and shuffled together some of the maps he had spread on the table. Then he set about extinguishing the candles before he left the library. The sky was beginning to lighten in the east as he made his way to his home near the town hall. He'd grab a couple of hours of shut-eye and then begin again.

Glen was dreaming again. The light was blinding, yet the colors were so vivid across the void in front of him. He was pretty sure he was floating in a sea of swirling sparkles so beautiful they brought tears to his eyes. And across the void, something more beautiful still: his wife, Sarah, dressed in flowing garments so brilliant that the colors hurt his eyes.

She came toward him, ever so slowly, and Glen ached to hold her in his arms. He attempted to go to her, but he couldn't move through the swirling light. He was floating, but it wasn't like water. There wasn't anything to swim through, it was like floating in space. He reached for her, but that was all he could do.

Sarah turned and gestured for him to follow her through a door, and then he was moving. It was like she held his tether and was reeling him in. He floated after her through the door, wanting to be with Sarah – to stay with Sarah. She was so beautiful, his lovely, special wife.

They were in his baby boy's bedroom, and on the floor three children were playing.

"Clarence," he said, tears catching in his throat.

They turned to look at him, but Clarence wasn't there after all. The faces belonged to Mia, Christian, and Sally. Confused, he tries calling Clarence's name again, but no sound came out of his mouth. He reached for them, but he was being pulled back from the room. The door closed in his face and then began melting away.

"Sarah!" he called, "Sarah, bring me with you!"

CHAPTER EIGHTEEN

MIA RAN THROUGH THE NIGHT. She avoided the game trail, crisscrossing her way up the hill. She figured as long as she was going up, she eventually would meet the game trail that led to the falls, and from there she could circle back to the rendezvous point. The problem was that it was hard to be quiet while crashing through the underbrush. She had scratches on her hands and face from overhanging branches, mud on her knees from tripping over vines and her palms were pained by every push. She didn't dare use her flashlight for risk of being spotted by her pursuers.

It took more than an hour to find the game trail, and when she did she wasn't certain which way to turn. It wasn't clear to her which direction the path had been when she'd headed into the woods. The fact that it was dark also wasn't helping her any. She stood indecisively for what seemed like forever, but probably was only a minute or two.

She took the trail to the right, thinking that if she hadn't reached the others in ten minutes, then she'd go the other direction. When ten minutes had gone by and she hadn't reached the others she hesitated. Had she gone far enough?

She decided on another five minutes just to be sure. But another five minutes on she still hadn't reached them. So, she reluctantly turned back, jogging along the trail, irritated that she'd wasted so much time.

She was so focused on the trail that Sally called out twice before Mia realized what she was hearing and changed direction, running down the Y toward the town. She found Sally kneeling next to Christian, who was slumped on the ground.

"Where's Glen?" Christian said through shallow breaths.

"Captured," Mia said. "We miscalculated, went into the pharmacy before your diversion and were captured. When the diversion came we were in the library and Glen made me run for it."

Christian groaned and Mia noticed a dark stain on his shirt, visible even in the dark. It reminded her of what they'd gone to the town for in the first place. She untied the bags from her belt and pulled a packet of capsules from her pocket.

"I've got the antibiotics," she said. "You need to take them. Glen made me memorize the dosages." She began popping the capsules from their foil pack. "Do we have anything he can swallow these with?" she asked Sally.

Sally produced a Camelback with a couple of inches of water in the bottom. The women helped Christian to raise his head and shoulders so he could swallow the medication.

"That's a lot of pills," Sally said. "Are you sure?"

"I'm sure," Mia replied. "I asked the same thing, but he needs to shock his system. We start big and slowly taper off. Here, help me with this."

They lowered Christian back down and pulled his shirt away from his wound. The sky had begun lightening, and Mia could see that the dressing Glen had applied to Christian's stomach was soaked with blood. She pulled it off and realized it wasn't just blood, but also pus. The gash was angry and red, with red streaks radiating from it.

"This is bad," she said to Sally, "really, really bad."

"I know it," Christian said. "Can you do anything?"

"Glen grabbed supplies and hid them for me to pick up," Mia said, thinking that accuracy wasn't the most important issue at the moment. "I'll see what he got for us." She opened one bag and then the other, sorting through the supplies.

"When my brother's toe got infected," Sally said, "the doctor made us soak it in Epsom salts so the infection would drain, but I don't know how to do that with the middle of a body."

"I've got saline," Mia said. "I'm going to squeeze as much of the pus out as I can. Then wipe it up with a sterile dressing, rinse it with saline and dry it, cover it in antibiotic ointment, and re-bandage it."

Sally looked at Mia, surprised, but Mia only shrugged.

"Glen made me memorize what to do," she said. "I had to recite it back to him about fifty times on the trip down the hill."

"He knew he wasn't going to make it out?" Sally asked, surprised.

"He wanted to cover all the bases," Mia said. She leaned over Christian. "This is going to hurt. I'm sorry, but there isn't any way around it."

Christian nodded and gritted his teeth as Mia began pressing on his abdomen. Large globules of stinking matter oozed across Christian's skin, and Sally had to turn away gagging. Mia wiped the majority of it away and looked to see how Christian was doing before she started again. He had passed out.

The fact that Christian was in and out of consciousness wasn't as helpful as Mia thought it might be. He groaned and thrashed when she began pressing again, making it difficult to keep pressure on the area.

"Sally, help me," she said. "You don't have to watch what I'm doing but go to his head and hold his shoulders down as best you can. I can't do this properly with him squirming and smacking at me like that."

"I'll try," Sally said, and went to Christian's head. She talked soothingly to him as she held him down, hoping her voice would calm him. "You really should be doing this part," Sally said. "He responds better to you."

"It can't be helped," Mia replied in exasperation, "I'm the one Glen explained this to. And I can't be cooing at him while I'm trying to save his life. There, no more pus is coming out now."

She wiped his skin again, opened a bottle of saline and flooded the wounded area with it. She patted him dry, applied ointment, and slapped a dressing over the wound. Then she got up and walked to the other side of the path, where she wretched. The smell was overwhelming and she couldn't get it out of her nose.

"Shouldn't we move him away from the path?" Sally asked. "They could find us here."

I don't want to disturb him right now," Mia said. "And besides, I'm too tired. I'd probably drop him on his head." She wandered to a patch of long weeds not far from where Christian was resting and curled up into a ball. "Wake me up if you hear someone coming."

Mia thought she would fall right asleep, but her mind kept going back to the moment when she had left Glen. She should have insisted he come with her. They could have outrun that lug who'd been sent back to watch them. She could have bashed him over the head with one of the big metal bookends that all were over the library. Why had she let Glen convince her to leave him behind? He'd seemed so sure at the time, so persuasive.

But now she was not at all sure she'd done the right thing. What if she hadn't done a good enough job on Christian's belly? If Glen had been here, he would have known if she'd been thorough enough. Christian's life was in her hands now, and she wished it wasn't. Why, oh why had she left Glen behind? It was clearly the wrong thing to do.

Mia buried her head under her arms and sobbed herself to sleep.

It was a dream she'd had many times before, the one where she always knew she was dreaming, but never could wake up, however much she wanted to do so. She and Sally were back at college, thinking it might be a safe place, with many resources. A place where the professors and administration would have been trained in emergency response and there would be routine and order.

There had been an order of sorts, a hierarchy of command that placed all students who remained in the role of servant. They'd gravitated toward student services, where the advisers had their offices, thinking that people who had degrees in psychology would have cooler heads. Would know how to keep people calm.

But their advisers had gone. The dream relived the same scene every time. She and Sally had been asked to see if they could get the generator started, even though they protested that they never even had seen a generator before. Together they'd climbed the metal ladder to the roof where the generator room was located. The rungs were hot and burned her bare hands. She should have asked if there were work gloves anywhere.

Heat waves radiated from the tar covering the roof and she was sweating before they reached the door to the generator room. Luckily, someone had left the padlock open so they didn't have to break in, but once in the generator room they were completely stymied. This is where the dream varied. Sometimes there had been no instructions, nothing to indicate the steps for starting the huge motor, just as it was that day. She and Sally had had to climb back down in defeat.

In this version of her dream, the room was empty, and Mia struggled to wake up. This was where the dream always became worse than what actually had happened. They searched the bare walls for a secret door or a sign that said what to do. They were examining the concrete slab, inch by inch, looking for something that would tell them what to do, when an adviser and her boyfriend from administration came in. Although in real life, they would not have climbed the steel ladder.

"Why haven't you started the generator yet?" the woman had whined at them. "Even an idiot could have started it by now." She turned to her boyfriend. "They always hire incompetents these days. The other custodian never took this long."

"It's ridiculous," he said, "we never should have let him leave. These stupid girls are no use."

Mia wanted to protest that the generator wasn't here, and they hadn't been given enough time to find it, but her mouth wouldn't open. The man grabbed Sally around the neck, dragged her across the roof, and pitched her over the side. The woman had hold of Mia's hair and was pulling her out of the room, backward. Mia resisted with every ounce of her strength, but the adviser was stronger than she was, and Mia was off-balance too.

She was pushed over the edge.

Mia awoke, sweating and breathing rapidly. The real memory of that day was fresh in her mind, the way it always was after the dream. The generator had been there, but they'd been unable to start it. The adviser and her boyfriend had screamed abuse and slapped Sally across her face. The boyfriend had said they were useless and should be ejected from the community.

"If you are so perfect," Mia had blurted out, "go up there and start it yourself."

"That's not my job." The adviser looked shocked. "I have other things to do."

"We have to keep things running," the man had said. "We have responsibilities. We can't be climbing roofs and starting generators, even though it would only take us a minute."

Another adviser had heard the ruckus and had come to lead her and Sally away. Sometimes in the dream, the adviser killed the pair in some particularly gruesome way. In real life, she and Sally had left the college that same day and she didn't know what had happened to the pair. She hoped they'd gotten what they deserved.

Now, she lay in deep shadow, the sun low on the horizon. She'd slept the entire day away. She looked around to see Sally helping Christian to drink some water. Pills! She'd forgotten his second dose of pills! She felt around in her pockets, becoming more and more panicked.

"I've got them," Sally called over. "He's had his second round."

Mia looked at her, confused. How did Sally know what Christian needed?

"You don't remember waking up, do you?" Sally asked. "You sat bolt upright around midday and told me not to forget Christian's capsules. You even told me how many and when. I guess your subconscious was worried you wouldn't wake up. Which you did not."

"Which I did not," Mia repeated. She couldn't believe she'd gone to sleep before making sure one of them could keep Christian on schedule.

"Hey," Sally said, "it's okay. You took care of it, and I

followed through. You don't have to beat yourself up over it."
She lowered Christian's head back to the ground.

"Do you think we could make it back to Glen's cabin?"
Sally asked. "Christian would be safer there while he heals."

"Maybe," Mia replied, "but I think we need to rescue
Glen and take him with us. He risked his life for Christian
and me."

"I don't think we can do that until Christian is better,"
Sally said. "We can't leave him sleeping in the woods. Another
bear could come along and kill him."

"I don't actually think a wild animal would come near him
while he smells of infection," Mia said. "They know better
than to eat infected flesh."

"I don't think that's true," Sally countered. "Wolves pick
off the weakest animals, often the sick or injured. And if they
are injured, they are bound to have an infection. And vultures
too. They'll eat anything."

"I'm not sure there are vultures around here," Mia said,
"but I guess we'd better not leave him behind. Although I'm
almost positive wild animals stay away from diseased flesh. I
took that class in wildlife biology, remember?"

"You were high in college," Sally said. "You probably aren't
remembering correctly."

"I was only high in the boring classes," Mia said. "Not
biology. I like biology."

"Well, I don't think we should leave Christian in any
case," Sally said. "What if he wakes up and is thirsty? Or has
to pee and walks over a cliff or something in his delirium?"

"I already said we wouldn't leave him," Mia said. "but that
doesn't solve the problem of where to stay while he's healing."

"I bet there are some empty houses around the town. You
know, a mile or two from the walls? We could stay there if we
didn't light a fire or have light at night. We'd be out of the
elements," Sally said.

"One of us would have to go on a scouting mission," Mia said. "We couldn't both go because of Christian."

"Duh," Sally said and pursed her lips. "You went into the town. So, I guess it's my turn to do the dangerous thing. Fair is fair."

"No. I think I'm better suited for scouting," Mia said. "I'm smaller and faster. Less likely to be seen."

"Less likely to be seen? Hah!" Sally snorted. "That hair of yours sticks out a mile. I just blend in." She ran her hand over her brownish hair. "And I can be really quiet and still when I need to be."

"But do you have the patience to sit and watch a house for hours at a time? You'll have to make sure no one is there before you enter." Mia squinted her eyes. "You aren't famous for measured decisions, you know."

"I can be as measured as you are," Sally said. "I do know what is at stake here. Anyway, Christian would be happier with you here. He worries about you."

"He worries about you too," Mia said. "And you can keep him calmer than I can."

Sally laughed.

"You'll say anything to keep me from going," she said. "You know that's not true."

Mia shrugged.

"Let's decide in the morning," she said. "There is no point in worrying about it now. It will be fully dark soon."

"All the more reason to decide tonight," Sally said. "One of us should be off at first light."

"We both can get up at first light, and then flip a coin or something," Mia said. "We shouldn't sleep while it's light out. Someone may come along and find us."

"True enough," Sally said. "But don't you dare get up and leave without waking me. We have to draw straws."

"Okay," Mia said. "I promise." But she already was

thinking of how to break the promise, without really breaking the promise. "We should wake up Christian and make him eat something, and give him his pills. How much of the bread do we have left?"

"I've got about four loaves," Sally said. "You?"

"Another four. And I know where Glen left his backpack, he's probably got some. I think we are okay for food. At least we won't starve to death yet. Although I'd really love something besides bread," Mia said.

"You know what I miss?" Sally asked. "Apple pie. I'm dying for some apple pie."

"Ice cream," Mia said with longing. "Chocolate ice cream in a really fresh sugar cone."

"I wonder if there is any chocolate left in the world?" Sally mused. "Do you think people who live where cocoa grows still can make chocolate?"

"Wouldn't do us any good," Mia said. "By the time it made the journey here it would be worth too much. We couldn't afford to barter for it."

"I know, but the thought of a world with no chocolate is too depressing. I wonder if we could get a seed and grow a plant indoors? How hard could it be?" Sally asked.

"I don't know," Mia said. "But I don't want to think about it. We need to wake Christian."

Mia helped Sally wake Christian and support him in a half-sitting position so he could swallow some food and medicine. She thought for a minute he was going to vomit it all up again, but he made an effort and kept it down. They laid him back on the grass and he was asleep immediately.

Mia lifted his shirt and removed the dressings. The wound was better than yesterday, thank goodness. The red streaks were shorter and had faded some. She pressed on the sides of the gash and, although pus still oozed from it, the volume had decreased. She took a deep breath and let out a sigh. The antibiotics were working.

"Is something wrong?" Sally asked, her eyebrows drawn together and fear in her eyes.

"No, for once something is going right," Mia said. She smiled at Sally, and turned her attention back to Christian, cleaning and re-bandaging his wound.

CHAPTER NINETEEN

WHEN MIA OPENED her eyes the next morning, Christian already was awake and sitting up. He smiled at Mia and put a finger to his lips, motioning to where Sally lay sleeping.

"Let's not wake her up," he whispered. "She was whimpering in the night. I think she's having bad dreams."

Mia understood about bad dreams only too well. She nodded and stretched, then rose quietly to find a spot in the woods to pee. Growing up, she never would have suspected that she'd one day be urinating in the woods with no toilet paper at hand. It was not a welcome change.

When she got back Sally still was asleep. So she sat close to Christian, leaning against him and offering him travel bread for breakfast. It had been so long since she'd last had coffee that her body no longer craved caffeine, but she still sometimes missed the ritual. The smell of the coffee brewing, stirring in cream and sugar, the bittersweet taste of the hot liquid on her tongue. She looked at the travel bread in her hand and tried to be grateful that she had something to eat.

"I was going to get up and leave you and Sally here," she

whispered to Christian. "But if you are well enough to travel, we should probably all stick together. What do you think?"

"I'm not sure how far we'll get," he said, "but I agree that we should stick together. Are you thinking of heading back to Glen's cabin?"

Mia shook her head. "We are going to look for an empty house somewhere not too far from the town," she said. "We want to rescue Glen."

"Do you think that is wise?" Christian asked. "We could get caught."

"We'll have to spend some time watching the town," Mia said. "But he saved your life and I think we owe it to him."

"We don't owe anyone anything." Christian snapped. "Haven't you listened to a word I've said? There is ruthless competition for resources. The only people you need consider are your family. That's you, me, and Sally now."

"And if it wasn't for Glen, it would just be me and Sally, because you'd be dead. He knew that we had come to take everything he had, and he helped us! I'm not willing to give up every bit of my humanity," Mia said, her voice rising.

"Nor am I," Sally said, sitting up and rubbing her eyes. "And he told us how to stop our periods. That's really big."

"Do we have to talk about women's private doings?" Christian asked, closing his eyes and shaking his head. "I don't want to hear it."

"I don't care what you want to hear," Sally said, getting up and pointing her finger at him. "If we don't have our periods, not only do we not have to improvise feminine hygiene products – and I'd like to see you have to do that -- but we can't get pregnant. That is potentially life-saving. I'd rescue Glen for that alone. But you," she shoved her finger in his direction, "would be dead! Isn't that worth something to you? You've never been risk-adverse before." She turned and stomped off into the woods.

Christian looked mutinous and Mia wondered if he would strike out for Glen's cabin on his own. Or if he even could find it. She was not sure she'd be able to make it back to Glen's place. There were too many twists and turns, and the woods all looked pretty much the same.

"Fine," she said to Christian, "you do what you want, but I'm going to help Glen. Reciprocity is what makes the world worth living in, if you ask me, which you didn't. When Sal is ready to go, we are taking off." She turned back to her backpack, stowing the things she lifted out when looking for the bread. She kept her head down, hoping he wouldn't see she was crying.

"Jesus Christ!" Christian exploded. "Where is your sense of self-preservation? You do know this is a suicide mission, don't you?"

"Not if we are smart about it," Mia said. "I made it out last time, didn't I? And I know what we are up against now. Which is more than I can say for you."

Mia didn't know why she was goading him. Christian was everything to her now, and she would not leave the man who had saved his life to languish and possibly die in that town. Christian didn't have to come with them, but if he didn't, she knew she might never see him again. She should be appealing to his honor, not shoving his face in her superiority. Shouldn't she?

"I'm ready," Sally said as she emerged from the undergrowth.

"You haven't eaten," Mia said.

"I can eat as we walk," Sally said. "Christian can't walk fast enough to give me indigestion."

"Christian is not coming," Mia said. "He's heading for Glen's cabin."

"I didn't say that," Christian countered angrily.

"Didn't you? That's what it sounded like to me," Mia

countered. "Your sense of self-preservation is fully intact. Right?"

"I don't think it's the wisest course of action," Christian said. "But if you won't come with me, then I'll have to go with you. I won't watch the two of you go off on your own. You might need me."

"I might need you?" Mia was indignant. "What about Glen? You know, the man who saved your life? He needs you."

"Just be happy I'm coming," Christian said, smiling at her. "And don't obsess about who I'm coming for. Gift horse." He raised an eyebrow at her.

"Fine. Let's get going then." She settled her pack on her back.

"What about Glen's pack?" Sally asked. "Shouldn't we bring it?"

"I don't see how we can," Mia said. "We each already have a pack to carry."

"Distribute the stuff between our three packs," Christian said, "and I'll carry his empty pack strapped to mine. We might need the stuff."

Mia dropped her pack to the ground and went off to find Glen's pack where they'd left it at the top of the trail. She dragged it back, it was uncommonly heavy, and started divvying up the contents.

"Wow," she said as she pulled the gun and ammunition from the pack, "no wonder this thing was so heavy."

"Did you know he brought a gun?" Sally asked. Her forehead was lined with worry.

"He was smart to bring a gun," Christian said. "He knew our plan was to murder him and take what we could. He was protecting himself."

"Do you think he would have killed us?" Sally asked.

"Why bother bringing us here if his plan was to kill us?" Mia asked. "Why not just kill us as we slept or something?"

"He was giving us a chance," Christian said. "He's a doctor. It's not in his nature to kill people. But if we had tried ambushing him once I was well? I think he would have done what he needed to protect himself from us." He took the gun and ammunition and put it in his own pack. "Can't blame him for that."

"We shouldn't have confessed," Sally said. "We should have pretended to be decent people." She took a third of the items from Glen's pack and stowed them in her own.

"Water under the bridge." Christian hoisted his pack. "Let's get moving."

The dream of Clarence's room still was vivid in Glen's mind, which was a little unusual. He thought about what it might mean. Why would Sarah lead him into a room where Christian, Mia, and Sally had taken the place of Clarence? Why hadn't she taken Glen with her? It was all that he wanted, to be with Sarah and Clarence again.

Of course, it didn't matter what he wanted. What mattered was what Sarah was trying to tell him. The trio still were just children and they needed him. It was the only thing that made sense. He was to teach them how to live without taking advantage of others. A self-reliant life without stealing and murdering. No taking advantage of people weaker than themselves. They must learn to live in the wilderness, where they won't be at the mercy of the more powerful, unscrupulous people. He had to save them.

He sat up carefully in the dark. He couldn't tell where he was or what dangers might lurk in the dark. His head was throbbing and he ached from lying on the hard floor. Wood, he thought, feeling the rough texture under his fingers. He reached out into space and felt nothing on the right, in front, or behind him. But on the left there was a wall. He moved his butt until his back was against the wall. He felt safer that way.

He sat until his head began to clear and the pain ebbed to tolerable levels. Then he stood cautiously but didn't come up against any obstacles. So far so good. Keeping one hand on the wall, he paced the circumference of the room, taking care to put each foot down before lifting the next, and to keep a hand out in front of him so he didn't run into anything. In this way he was able to discover that he was in an apparently empty room of approximately eight by ten feet. There was a door midway along one of the long walls, but no light penetrated the space around the edges. He didn't know if that was because the door was fitted with a light blocking seal, or because it was nighttime.

Then because his head was pounding, and he felt dizzy and queasy again, he sat back down. He was hungry, thirsty and needed to pee. He wasn't sure if the unruly state of his stomach was due to the need to eat or the blow to his head. He leaned his head against the wall and hoped they weren't going to starve him to death. That was a horrible way to die.

A memory of Clarence came to him. They'd vacationed on the central coast of California the year Clarence was two, the summer before he'd lost them both. Clarence stood at the edge of the ocean, his arms spread as if to take it all in, wonder reflected in his face. He'd run to the water, squealing when the waves washed in and licked his toes.

They'd spread their blanket on the sand, although they might as well have just sat in the sand. Clarence shoveled sand and it went everywhere, including Glen's mouth. The wind whipped Sarah's hair across her face and she laughed when Clarence tried burying Glen in the sand.

Glen felt himself smiling at the memory of Sarah giving Clarence crackers to feed the seagulls. The birds swooped down and snatched the food from his fingers in full flight. Clarence clapped and laughed, then asked for another cracker. They fed more to the seagulls than they ate that day.

They'd walked the shore, Clarence running in and out of the waves, picking up shells and seaweed, pebbles, and handfuls of wet sand. Sara told him that crabs lived under the bubbles in the beach. Clarence had fallen sound asleep on his towel and Glen had carried him back to the car as evening fell, the wind beginning to carry a chill.

It occurred to Glen that he was thinking of water because of the need to relieve himself. He may have to choose a corner and use it as a toilet. But he'd wait for now, in fact, until he couldn't wait any longer. He'd rather not resort to animal behavior if he didn't have to do so.

He pictured Sarah, smiling on the beach, strands of her hair coming loose from her ponytail and flying around her head. She'd held his hand and kissed him as Clarence slept, promising more when they returned to the hotel. He physically ached for her, his throat constricting and his heart contracting. Sarah, take me with you, he thought.

The door opened, and he was blinded by sunlight streaming through the doorway. There was a figure backlit in the door. An empty bucket was dropped inside the threshold, a water bottle tossed at his feet, and a paper bag tossed in his lap. Then the door closed and he was in the dark again. He hadn't even thought to look around his prison while the door had been open.

If they'd been able to travel by the paths and road it would have taken no time at all to walk the few miles from town that they'd wanted to be. But they couldn't risk being seen, so they picked their way through the undergrowth. Mia had scrapes on her arms and ankles from the thistles and briers. She had scratches on her face and leaves in her hair from low hanging branches. All in all, she wasn't in the best of moods.

"Come on, Mia," Christian barked at her. "We need to cover more ground."

At that moment Sally brushed past a branch that snapped

back and hit Mia square in the face, knocking her flat on her back. She lay on the ground swearing, not even bothering to try getting up.

Sally appeared above her, looking concerned. "Oh my God, Mia, I'm so sorry. Are you alright?"

"I'm fine," Mia grumbled, struggling out of her backpack so she could stand up. She felt her cheek and her hand came back bloody.

"Great." It was quite a lot of blood, which meant she'd probably have a scar on her face. Not that it mattered anymore, but still. She struggled not to cry.

Christian came to stand next to Sally. Mia noticed his face was white and pinched. "You need to rest," Mia said. "You're in pain."

"What I need to do is clean up that cut on your face," Christian said. "You don't want it to scar. Sit on that log."

He got out the first aid kit and set about cleaning and dressing the wound. Mia saw the worry in his eyes and wondered how bad it must be. It stung when he sprayed disinfectant on it and she bit her lip. If he could handle her squeezing pus from his belly, then she could handle this. But she was relieved when the bandage went on.

Christian sat next to her on the fallen log. Sally dropped her backpack on the ground and perched on it. Christian let out a sigh. "I wish there was an easier way to travel," he said. "Hacking our way through the undergrowth like this is exhausting."

"Your face is gray," Mia said. "We'd better stop for a few minutes. And I should look at your stomach again."

"My stomach is fine," Christian said through clenched teeth. "We need to keep moving."

"Humor me," Mia said. "Let me look, and then we can get moving again."

Christian grunted and lifted his shirt. Blood soaked his dressing, but there was no sign of infection.

"You are bleeding again," Mia said as she pulled some butterfly strips from the first aid kit. "You need to be more careful or you'll pass out from losing too much blood. It's not like we can stop by the local corner store and buy you some plasma." She cleaned the wound and closed the area that was leaking with the butterflies. She covered the area with a thicker dressing and taped it down. She looked up at his face, which was drawn and cold-looking.

"Do you understand?" she asked. "You need to take it easy. We can't rescue Glen if we're spending all our time keeping you alive."

Christian nodded. "Yeah, okay," he said. "Thirty-minute rest before moving on again."

"Good," Mia said, and dropped to the ground. "Wake me up in thirty minutes."

"Shouldn't one of us keep watch?" Sally asked.

Mia grunted her assent. Her intention had been to drift off to sleep to escape the pain in her face, but she didn't drift. The ground was hard and there was a rock jabbing her butt. Her face still stung. She felt like she could cry, but didn't want to because then she'd have to deal with sympathy from Sally and Christian. She tried breathing through the pain, but her cheek stung and burned.

Mia opened her eyes and reached for the first aid kit that still was on the ground beside her. She rolled onto her side and opened it, searching for some kind of pain relief. There wasn't any over the counter medication anywhere that she could see, but there was morphine and codeine and a handy dosage guide.

She remembered taking codeine when she had her wisdom teeth out and didn't remember it having the kind of kick she needed now. So, she pulled out a syringe and an ampoule of morphine. She read the dosage instructions carefully and drew the appropriate amount in through the needle and injected it into her thigh.

It seemed like her vision began to blur almost immediately, which didn't alarm her until she realized her chest was tightening and her heart was beating wildly. She clutched at her throat, trying to get air in her lungs but failing. The world was blurry and unstable, so she closed her eyes. She heard Sally yelling her name, and then Christian, so far away. She was going, sinking into the ground, she thought. Maybe even dying.

Mia opened her eyes to find Christian and Sally bending over her, calling her name. "I'm alive," she croaked. "How'd that happen?"

"Did you inject morphine?" Christian asked angrily. He was shaking with rage.

"My face was burning," Mia said. "I had to do something."

"You had a reaction," Sally said. "Didn't you know you were allergic?"

"I've never had morphine before," Mia said. "I didn't even know you could be allergic to it." She rubbed her thigh. "Why does my leg hurt?" she asked.

"We had to inject you with epinephrine so you wouldn't die," Christian said. "It packs a punch. You'll probably have a hell of a bruise."

"Yeah," Mia said, laying her head down on the ground. Can I have a few minutes to rest before we start going again?" She was feeling very fuzzy.

"We'll need to stay the night here." Christian's voice was muffled. "She won't be worth anything for at least twenty-four hours."

Mia was pretty sure he was talking to Sally, which was good. She couldn't have answered if she'd wanted to do so.

CHAPTER TWENTY

Terror was pacing the library. His pulse was pounding in his temples and he was having trouble containing his rage. How dare they question his motives, his decisions? Wasn't he the leader here? Wasn't he the one who had brought them security and peace? He should kill them now. All of them. There were plenty of people in this world dying to live in security.

He remembered the scene at the fire. It had been an old pickup, not used anymore and in a place that posed no danger to the buildings. They'd wanted to track the vandals, but Terror would not let them. He'd explained that he had the doctor, and the others were not important, but they would not listen. Now he would kill them all.

No, not all of them, just one. But who?

He quickened his pace, slamming his fist on a table as he passed. He loved the feel of the library, the wood and books. The antique light fixtures that hung from the high ceiling reminded him of libraries the world round. Places of solitude and learning. Hushed places where he could think, consider what needed to be done, and where he could plan in peace.

But now it felt too tame. He needed a war room. A place he could order his men to bring him one of the ring leaders. Or better still, one of their wives.

He stopped short, wavering a little, his head refusing to stop its spinning and pounding.

He would kill one of the women. A cold calmness finally spread over him. Yes. That would teach them. He'd tried to be fair, but he couldn't have them questioning his decisions. He wouldn't let them undermine him. But why lose one of the men? He needed his warriors, and very few of them were women.

The face of a tall brunette came to mind. She had spurned him. Refused to cheat on her man. How dare she? He'd played it cool at the time. He'd let her walk away. But he hadn't forgotten the look of contempt she'd given him. Her words had been like a slap in the face. She'd questioned his loyalty to his men. Said he was no more than a boy slut.

She would pay for that now.

Calm now, he sat in his favorite armchair at the head of a long table. He leaned back and crossed his feet on the table and thought about how this would go down. He'd gather the townspeople at the town square. He'd praise the fire brigade for their quick work on the burning truck. He'd tell the town how fortunate they were to have a surgeon. He'd have the doctor cleaned up and present him to the town. Offer him the pick of the empty houses.

Then he'd call for the families of the men who had questioned him. He'd reprimand the men, then tell them he had decided to spare them. Then he would explain that he couldn't have them second-guessing his decisions, and to make sure it never happened again, he was going to take one of their women. He'd call for that bitch, he couldn't remember her name, and when her man challenged him he'd shoot her in the face.

He could imagine this man, Charro was his name, saying, "I won't let you touch my woman." And he, Terror, would say, "I wouldn't be caught dead touching that whore." And then when they were looking at him in confusion he would kill her. And in the chaos of crying women and children, the men gathering them into safety, he, Terror, would walk away calmly. That should keep them from questioning him again.

He would bring them to their knees.

He took a deep breath and relaxed. His head had stopped pounding, the rage had melted away. He was feeling good. Powerful. Hadn't he caught them a healer of the first rank? Yes, he had. What he needed now was a woman. He thought about his Angelica, one of his best officers. But she was too feisty for his current mood. It was like trying to make love to a wild cat. He would come away looking like he'd wrestled a bear. No, what he wanted was someone submissive. Someone who could take some punishment without giving it back.

He thought of the women in town, married and single alike, and as he thought he found himself getting hard. He got up and shrugged on his leather jacket, blew out the candles, and strode out of the building. He'd go down to the pub and see who was feeling the need to be dominated.

Terror awoke the next morning next to a woman with fresh bruises on her face and upper arms and was struck with self-loathing. He did not remember the night before, but he had no doubt that he had been the one to inflict the damage. She whimpered as he slipped out of bed. Waking in pain, he quickly moved, not wanting to face her.

He dressed quickly and slipped out of the room. Then he went into the bathroom and looked in the mirror. He had scratches down his face. What had he done? This wasn't the first time he'd hurt someone with no memory of it happening. Apparently, this time she had fought back. Good for her.

He cleaned himself up and went downstairs to where his men were waiting.

"Go find the doctor," he said to Mike.

"He's drunk," Mike said. "But I'll bring him if you want."

"No," Terror said. "Get the surgeon we have locked in the closet over in Angelica's place. He's not drunk."

Mike got up and left the room, leaving Ed and Jackal playing cards at the table. He considered Ed was probably the least objectionable to a woman.

"Ed," he said, "go upstairs and wake the girl. Make sure she cleans herself up. Help her if she needs it."

"Is she going to smack me like the last one?" Ed asked.

"Possibly," Terror said, "but how much damage do you think she can do? You might have a red mark on your face."

"Great," Ed said, but he stood up and went upstairs.

Glen was refusing to use the bucket as a toilet. Not that he'd really have a choice if they left him here alone much longer. He'd eaten the bread his visitor had tossed in his lap, and drank most of the bottle of water. But use the bucket as a toilet he would not.

He was wondering how much longer he could hold out when the door opened and a man's voice said, "Let's go."

Glen thought he recognized the voice from the pharmacy, but he wasn't sure which of the men it was. He stood up, steadied himself, and moved into the light, blinking.

They let him use the facilities, handed him an old-fashioned doctor's bag, and led him out of the building.

It turned out he'd been locked in a walk-in closet on the second floor of a home on Main Street. As he passed through the front hallway he got glimpses of whitewashed wood, and bright-colored throw pillows and blankets, and the smell of wood smoke, fresh bread and apples scented the air. Then he was outside and being hurried down the brick walkway to the sidewalk.

The spots of lawn that hadn't been turned into vegetable patches all were trim and neat, and that surprised Glen, until he saw a teenaged boy pushing a reel mower. He wondered where they had found that. Michigan wasn't exactly known for non-motorized garden implements.

He was marched up Main Street and then right up a side street to a modest home in a less affluent neighborhood. The lawns still were tidy, and the homes painted and in good repair, but Glen would have placed money on there being no whitewashed rooms inside. White paint on sheet rock, maybe, but no real wood-paneled rooms with brightly colored throw pillows and blankets. These were working people's houses.

He was led up the walkway to one of the larger homes. They didn't knock but just walked right in the door, through the entry, and into the room on the right. It was a comfortable living room, with neutral walls and matching furniture. Terror was standing, looking out the front window. The man named Mike from the pharmacy was sitting in a chair across from a young woman who was perched on the couch, hugging herself. The woman had her eyes on the floor, but Glen could see she wore some pretty nasty bruises on her face and arms.

"You're here," Terror said flatly. "We are in need of your professional services."

"You lock me in a dark closet and then pull me out to demand my services?" Glen was having trouble keeping his rising anger in check. "Why exactly should I help you?"

"This woman is injured," Terror said. He was looking out the window again, talking with his back to Glen and the others. "Our family doctor is stinking drunk. I could wait until he sobers up, but meanwhile she is in pain. You can stand on your principles, I suppose. But she will suffer for it."

Glen blanched. Putting it that way, he'd be a prick not to

help her. He stood up. "We'll need a private room," he said. "Soap and hot water.

He followed Third Eye and the girl to a room down the hall, waited until Mike delivered the supplies he needed, and then closed the door on the men.

"What's your name?" he asked the girl, but she just shook her head.

"Can you tell me how this happened?"

Again, a shake of the head but nothing more. He yanked the top sheet off the twin bed in the corner of the room. "Get undressed," he said, "and wrap yourself in this. I'll be outside the door, so just knock when you are ready, and I'll come in."

By the time he'd finished his exam, he was livid. The woman, hell, she wasn't much more than a girl really, needed x-rays. He suspected that under the bruising she had a broken cheekbone, ribs, and wrist. That she had been sexually assaulted was all too clear, even if the girl wouldn't let him do a proper exam. He told her to stay put and marched into the living room.

"That girl needs a woman to help her get cleaned up and dressed," he announced to the men in the room. Terror waved his hand and Mike got up and left the room.

"I need to take x-rays of her wrist, ribs, and face," Glen continued. "I don't know which one of you did this, but if it happens again and I'm still a prisoner in this town, I will kill the one who did. Do you understand? I have no problem killing a man who would rape and beat a woman, and this one is little more than a child." He stopped to see if the men took his meaning, but all three stared at him blankly.

"What is wrong with you?" Glen heard his voice rise in anger. "Are you that far gone?"

"What you don't realize, Doc," Terror said, "is that we've

seen far worse. Will her fractures heal without x-rays? If indeed she does have fractures?"

"They will heal," he said, fuming. "But they'd heal better if I could be sure they were set correctly and cast."

"You would cast her face?" Third Eye laughed. "I'd like to see that."

"I'm talking about her ribs and her wrist," Glen said. "They should be seen to."

"What did she tell you about what happened to her?" Terror asked.

The change in subject confused Glen. What was Terror up to?

"Nothing. She told me nothing," he said. "Not one word passed her lips."

A fleeting look of relief passed over Terror's face, which incensed Glen.

"Listen, I know you have the facilities and the power for me to take an x-ray. Why ask me to look at the girl and then block me from doing what needs to be done? It makes no sense." Glen was beginning to think Terror had multiple personality disorder. He was clearly unhinged.

"Let me take care of the girl," he shouted and then calmed himself. "Some of the injuries are clearly sexual in nature. It's possible if there was a woman in the room she might let me tend to them. Can you arrange that?"

He felt as if he were talking to a wall. Terror clearly was not interested in the girl's welfare beyond very basic health-care and her desire to keep her mouth shut. Why even bother to call him in? And was it Terror who had inflicted those wounds? If so, he was a lot worse that Glen had thought. And if he was covering up for someone, well, that was bad too.

"Can you give her something to keep her from getting pregnant?" Terror asked.

"It depends on what you have in your pharmacy, but yes, I

can if she wants me to do that." Glen thought it would be a wise precaution but wouldn't force the girl to take any medication if she didn't want to do so.

Terror nodded to Third Eye, "Take him to the pharmacy. Let him take what he needs." Then he turned to Boss Man, "Make sure she stays here until the doctor gets back," Terror said.

Third Eye gestured to the door and Glen followed him out into the sunshine. It was a five-block walk and Glen kept his eyes open. Instead of marveling at the technology that kept the town running, he looked for possible escape routes.

In the pharmacy, he quickly found what he needed and then used his memory of the supply shelves to pocket a few other useful items, all the while making Third Eye think he couldn't find what he was looking for. Third Eye, for his part, was rummaging through the stock in the main store and not paying any attention to Glen. Glen was thoughtful about his choices. He didn't have Christian to worry about. He'd either be on his way to recovery or dead by now. Glen hoped it was recovery, but in either case it was no longer his concern.

He thought about what he might need while imprisoned in a closet, and what would be useful if he ever got out of this place. Practicality played a part as well. If he couldn't slip it in his pocket, it was out of the question and clearly if it had to be refrigerated, there was no point in taking it. Painkillers, antibiotics, anti-bacterial cream, wound care supplies, and upset stomach medicine all were useful things that he'd thrown in a bag the first time he was in here. That bag was either with Mia and the others or had been found and the items returned.

He finally told Third Eye he'd found what he needed, and they headed back to Terror's house. Again, Glen kept his eyes open. He noticed a railroad track and wondered if that would be a viable escape route. Then he wondered about the train cars. What had happened to the locomotives when their chips had burned out? And what about the steam trains? Were they viable? Was anyone using them to clear the tracks and move people and things across the country?

They reached the house and Glen pulled his attention back to the task at hand. He'd have to be on his toes to convince Terror to let him treat the girl. The inconsistencies in Terror's personality bothered Glen. Why bring Glen into it all if he wasn't going to be allowed to treat her injuries? Why spare Glen, but allow others to be killed? There was a disconnect in logic that bothered Glen. He didn't like what he was seeing.

Terror was gone when they got back, and in his place was an older woman, possibly in her sixties. She was sitting in the armchair, knitting, but she put it aside and stood when Glen and Third Eye entered.

"Hello," the older woman said, "you must be the doctor. Shall we get started?"

Glen followed her down the hall. He was thinking he'd already started, but he didn't say anything. There was no point in antagonizing people who were helping him.

The young woman was back in the room, sitting on the bed in a hospital gown. She'd had a bath, her hair was wet and dripping down her back, and the smell of soap wafted off her. The older woman clucked her tongue, took the towel from the foot of the bed and scrunched the girl's wet hair with it.

"What's your name?" Glen asked. "I can't just call you 'Woman'."

"You can call her Anna," The older woman said. "Isn't that right, Anna?"

Anna nodded.

"And what may I call you?" he asked the older woman.

"Mrs. Smith," she said.

"Okay, Anna, I have some questions for you. Is it okay if Mrs. Smith stays with you for this part?" he asked.

Anna nodded. This was going to be a long question and answer question session if she only was going to communicate in nods.

As it turned out, Anna would not open her mouth. Not to answer a question and not to let him look inside. He had to pry one hand from around the other wrist. She moaned and grit her teeth as he felt the bone as gently as he could and still couldn't tell anything. She would not let him perform a gynecological exam. She clutched her gown and clenched her knees together, shaking her head violently.

"I could make you feel more comfortable, and avoid infection..." he petered out. She was shaking her head violently.

"Give me the medicine and the instructions," Mrs. Smith said. "She may let me do what she won't let you do."

"I won't know what she needs until I can look and see what the damage is," Glen said. "But I can give you some general advice that won't do damage regardless of what's wrong." Glen's frustration was growing. It was clear that Anna had been abused by someone, and how was he supposed to treat her? He asked Mrs. Smith for warm water and wrapped Anna's wrist in a cast. He supported it until it hardened.

Then he gave Anna the morning-after pill packet and explained how to use it. She nodded and popped the pills from the foil pack as Mrs. Smith handed her a glass of water.

"You can get dressed now," he said. "I'd still really like to x-ray that wrist and your face, but there's no guarantee I'll get permission."

"See if you can get her to change her mind about me," he said to Mrs. Smith as he left the room. "She really should be thoroughly examined."

But he knew he was wasting his breath. That girl never was going to let him examine her.

As they led him back to his closet on the other side of Main Street, Glen noticed the sunlight was turning that funny color that it did sometimes before a storm. He wondered if it was going to be a bad one.

The rain awakened Mia. It beat steadily on her head and she might have wondered what was going on if she hadn't felt it running down her face. She picked up her head and looked around. She still was in the spot where she had collapsed earlier. All the backpacks were piled nearby, but neither Sally nor Christian were anywhere to be seen. She rummaged through their things until she found the bivy tent. She set it up where it had some protection from overhanging branches.

She pulled all the packs inside and laid back down on the tent floor. Her clothes were soaked and she knew she should change, but she needed to rest. Her face hurt and she didn't feel right. Maybe it was a reaction to the morphine and the epinephrine. She didn't know. She wanted to sleep, but the cut on her cheek made it impossible to find a comfortable position. Putting weight on her cheek made it hurt like hell, but when she tried the other side the lack of pressure brought another kind of pain. She didn't dare try any kind of painkiller, because Lord knows she didn't want to go through that again.

Rain was pinging off the tent and the wind had started to pick up. The temperature was dropping and she hoped Christian and Sally were safe. She wriggled out of her wet clothes and pulled on dry things, adding a jacket for warmth. She wondered if the tent could blow away with her in it.

With nothing to do to take her mind off her thoughts the worry escalated. And she found herself rocking where she sat, her breathing shallow. "Stop this right now," she said aloud.

"There's no point working yourself into a lather, you'll be no use to anyone."

At that moment, the tent flap unzipped and a dripping Sally came in. Her hair was not only dripping but looked like it had been styled with a blender. Mia scooted back to give her some room in the cramped tent.

"Who were you talking to?" Sally asked. "I thought Christian must be in here with you, which made no sense because the plan was for me to get back first."

"I was just talking to myself," Mia said. "As you do, you know, when you're alone and you don't know where your companions are."

"You were out cold," Sally said, "and your breathing and heartbeat were steady. So, we decided to do a recon and see if we were close to any buildings. I didn't find any, but I have a feeling I was walking in circles. I've got to change."

Sally pulled off her clothes and added them to Mia's pile of soggy things. Then she pulled on dry clothes and pulled the sleeping bag off her pack and unzipped it. "Come on," she said, "snuggle up. We need to stay warm. The wind out there was wicked. I'm glad you thought to get the bivy up."

"The rain woke me up," Mia said. "It seemed like the logical thing to do. When are we expecting Christian back?"

"I think he was probably thirty minutes farther out than I was. So, I don't know, maybe another thirty minutes?" Sally said.

But night fell and Christian didn't return. Mia felt the old anxiety rising in her chest and had to remind herself to breathe. The wind buffeted the tent, making it vibrate around them in a way that unsettled Mia. Sally drew the sleeping bag closer around them and started humming lullabies. Mia knew she was doing it to calm her. She didn't know if she should be offended for being treated like a child, or grateful that she had a companion who noticed her discomfort and tried to help.

"Do you remember that guy from chemistry that you had a crush on?" Mia asked.

"Yeah," Sally said, "what made you think of him?"

It was the rain that made me think of him," Mia said. "The last time I saw him he was standing in the rain outside the university library, staring up at the third floor window."

"I used to study on the third floor," Sally said. "In the window alcove. Do you think he was looking at me?"

"I didn't know if you were there or not that day, but yeah, I think he was pining after you."

"How funny," Sally said, "I wish I'd known. I haven't thought of him for a long time."

"Me neither," Mia said. "I wonder if he is still alive?"

"Oh. I hope so. I'd hate to think I'd missed my chance completely," Sally said. "Did you have a crush at college?"

"Yeah, but it was an associate professor. I didn't have a chance in hell with him. He was surrounded by graduate students."

"What was he a professor of?" Sally asked. "Do you remember?"

"Anthropology," Mia sighed. "Such a lovely class. We were studying the different ways cultures are put together. The female polygamous cultures of Nepal were my favorite, until I learned that the women didn't really have a choice. Marry one brother and you marry them all."

"Why do they do that?" Sally asked.

"Shortage of land. That way the boys all stay in one house and the land doesn't have to be divided. And no one knows whose son is whose, so they just grow up with however many fathers."

"I don't think I'd like that," Sally said. "I think it would be better to have many wives and one husband. That way you wouldn't have to spend too much time with the guy, and you'd always have women around to help with chores and to talk to. You could compare your husband's performance."

"I don't think the Nepalese live like that anymore anyway," Mia said. "The modern world has caught up with them."

"That's too bad," Sally said. "It's the end of a way of life. The death of a culture."

"I suppose so," Mia said, "but I can't help thinking it's better for the women. Can you imagine having to have sex with the older brother all the time, when it was the middle or younger brother who you were in love with? Ugh."

"Are you hungry?" Sally asked. "I have some travel bread in my pack."

They shared a loaf of travel bread and some water, and then snuggled together under the sleeping bag for warmth. They fell asleep hoping Christian was okay.

It still was raining when Mia awoke early the next morning. It barely was light out, and she wondered what had woken her. Well, worried more than she wondered, if the truth be told. She really should still be asleep.

"Come on, you two," came Christian's voice from outside the tent. "Time to get up."

"It's still storming. Can't we wait until it dries up outside?" Mia said. "I'm cold."

Sally stirred and mumbled.

"It's not storming," Christian said, "just raining. The wind has stopped."

"But it's still wet out there," Mia moaned, "and Sally is asleep."

"I'm awake," Sally mumbled, audibly this time. "Is that you, Christian?"

"Yes, it's me. Get up, you lazy creatures. It's time to get moving," he said.

"It's barely even light," Sally said. "Come in and lie down for a while. You've been out all night. You need to rest."

"I'm all wet," he said. "I don't think you'd like me crawling into bed with you, but if you insist." He started to unzip the tent fly.

"No," Mia cried. "No wet men in the tent. I've used up all my dry clothes." She groaned and untangled herself from the sleeping bag. "This better be good." She pulled on her still damp shoes.

"Don't go, Mia," Sally pleaded. "If you go, I have to go, and I'm not awake yet."

"Come on, Sal," Christian said. "I promise you it will be worth it."

"These are my only dry clothes too," Sally whined. "If I come out there, they won't be dry anymore."

"It won't matter," Christian said, "because we'll be able to dry them. Come on, you lazy sods, I've found us a house."

"Really?" Mia asked. "And no one is living there?" She pulled on her boots in earnest now.

"I spent all afternoon watching it," Christian said. "And I spent the night inside it. I'm fairly certain no one is living there. And it's only a couple of miles from the town, but far enough from the road to be overlooked."

"Okay," Sally said. "I'm coming. But I'd better be able to dry my clothes when we get there."

———

FIND out what happens in part two! Available Now!